BBQ DELIVERED WITH ATTITUDE

BBQ DELIVERED WITH ATTITUDE

THE UNBELIEVABLE MR. BROWNSTONE™ BOOK TWENTY

MICHAEL ANDERLE

DISRUPTIVE IMAGINATION

LMBPN Publishing
PMB 196, 2540 South Maryland Pkwy
Las Vegas, NV 89109

First US edition, September 2019
Version 1.01, December 2019
ebook ISBN: 978-1-64202-448-7

Special Thanks
to Mike Ross
for BBQ Consulting
Jessie Rae's BBQ - Las Vegas, NV

Thanks to the JIT Readers

Jeff Eaton
Dave Hicks
Jeff Goode
Nicole Emens
Micky Cocker
Shari Regan
Peter Manis
John Ashmore
Larry Omans
Deb Mader
Diane L. Smith
James Caplan
Dorothy Lloyd
Paul Westman
Kelly O'Donnell

If I've missed anyone, please let me know!

Editor
Lynne Stiegler

*To Family, Friends and
Those Who Love
to Read.
May We All Enjoy Grace
to Live the Life We Are
Called.*

CHAPTER ONE

The F-350 barreled down the highway. Traffic was light for late afternoon. Chatter filled the truck's cabin from two barbeque podcast hosts discussing different spice and meat pairings. It was another normal day for James Brownstone.

"I'm telling you, Jill," one of the hosts began, "you'd be surprised how well cardamom works in the recipe. I was shocked and stunned by the deliciousness."

Jill laughed. "Okay, Henry. You've convinced me. I'll try cardamom the next time I make that brisket."

James' experiences in Colorado the previous fall had convinced him that he needed to push a little harder to explore the fundamental nature of barbeque. He'd never been against testing the boundaries, but since opening his own place, he had let himself fall into an easy pattern of obsessing over the same preferred recipes. They were damned good recipes, but the same ones, nonetheless. While he was going to respect the basics of his craft and not go too crazy, he wanted to expand his scope of barbeque appreciation.

He chuckled. Some days, his old life felt like it belonged to a different man who just happened to have his name and look exactly like him. While he had always enjoyed barbeque, he had spent too much time beating down scummy bounties to worry about mastering his core styles, let alone exploring fringe techniques and proteins. Now, he had plenty of time to work in the restaurant and appreciate his family. Semi-retirement wasn't such a bad thing.

The Lord had provided. This was what his life was always meant to be. He ran a good restaurant that contributed a solid effort to the LA barbeque scene. His beautiful, ass-kicking wife was about to give birth, and his daughter was doing well for herself, even if the occasional mysterious and dangerous organization went after her.

The constant concern over Alison's safety that had plagued James for years was now a mere background murmur in his thoughts. Alison had long since proven she could handle herself, and she'd done it again with the Tapestry. If anything, the range of her magical abilities meant she could deal with a lot of problems he'd have more difficulty handling. Kicking ass by slicing a guy's head off or stomping through a window was straightforward, but not every problem in life could be resolved by the extreme application of force.

She'd even found a good man. James would never fully be comfortable with her getting married, but Mason was a solid pick. He would always have Alison's back both professionally and personally.

Shit. They're not gonna be engaged forever, which means I could end up a grandfather in a few years.

James didn't know what to make of that idea. It'd probably bother Shay more than him. He'd never felt young even when he was a kid.

Worrying less about Alison meant James had fully enshrined KISS as the top priority in his life again, at least until the baby was born. All the child-rearing podcasts he'd been listening to since Shay had told him the news had made it very clear that the baby would dictate the new terms of his daily existence, and it'd be at least a couple of years before he could start anything approaching proper training.

Shay insisted it'd be far longer than a couple of years before she wanted their kid running around preparing to be a Brownstone, but James didn't see anything wrong with a toddler-scale tactical obstacle course. Wasn't that just promoting physical play and well-being?

It wasn't like he was planning to give the kid a weapon. If Alison could begin training while she was still blind, her new sibling could start once he or she learned to walk and jump. Every pediatrician said exercise was good for kids. Parents who were *not* sending their kids through tactical obstacle courses were the ones who should be defending themselves.

Six weeks remained until the baby would be born, and James intended to live the simple life as much as possible until then. The incident last fall with Nadina aside, he hadn't had to worry about much other than Shay or barbeque in months. An occasional quick trip with the agency to beat down bounties helped keep Whispy from complaining too much, and only the dimmest of idiots dared to even shoot an angry look his way. The idea of someone blowing up his house again was ludicrous. Even the Vax understood they needed to stay the hell away, and half the galaxy was terrified of *them*. They had just accepted who the bigger badass was.

James smiled.

My new kid will grow up with a loving family who can kick anyone's ass if they screw with them, but I'll make sure the kid knows how to kick butt, too, just in case. When they're old enough, they're going to start doing summers either at the agency or Alison's company.

How early? Is ten too early? Twelve? I'll have to talk to Shay about it, but she's already complaining about the obstacle course. Maybe if I mention tomb raids, she'll see it my way.

It wasn't as if he intended to pressure his new child into any particular career path. Bounty hunter, security consultant, or tomb raider were all fine. The only thing he refused to budge on was a proper food education. The child would learn intricacies of barbeque from the second they had teeth. They didn't have to love his preferred styles, but they would know barbeque.

About the only thing I won't allow is a vegetarian.

Farther up the road, a large truck jerked and swerved before falling onto its side. James slammed his foot on his brake pedal, his hands tightening on the wheel. The F-350's tires squealed and the vehicle shook.

Damn.

The crashing truck ahead sparked as it scraped along the concrete. Metal, plastic, and glass chunks shot into the air and rained down on the nearby lanes. A closely-trailing

SUV slammed on its brakes and veered hard to the left, desperate to avoid the fallen truck, but clipped its side. The blow launched the SUV onto its side, and it skidded along the road, smashing through a guard rail and dropping into the narrow plant-covered median. The SUV smacked into a palm tree, and the impact halted the vehicle but uprooted the tree. It fell onto its side, blocking another lane. The quick and careful response of the drivers in that lane avoided another accident. Maybe it was a convoy of Gray Elves.

Several other vehicles on James' side of the median had better luck than the SUV. Their brake lights lit almost in unison, the tires of the cars and trucks leaving black streaks on the concrete. A sedan that had been right behind the SUV came to a stop a few yards away from the initial overturned truck. The other cars formed an uneven glob around it as they stopped, James' F-350 at the outer edge of the main highway clot. The vehicles behind slowed to a stop in the halted lanes, not an abnormal sight in greater Los Angeles, even without traffic accidents.

The passenger-side door of the overturned truck opened and the driver crawled out, grimacing. His face was bloodied, and one of his feet bent at an unnatural angle. A few people emerged from their cars and rushed over to the truck to help him down. They carried him toward a nearby parked car.

A moment later, two men jogged toward the SUV but hesitated as flames and sparks from the front of the vehicle lit the shrubs, grass, and trees in the surrounding area on fire.

It's always something in LA. All this magic in the world, and we still have to deal with traffic accidents.

James shrugged off his coat and reached under his shirt to yank off the spacer separating his amulet from his chest. He hissed as the tendrils shot into his flesh, the pain familiar but still intense after all these years. He took a few deep breaths, now fully bonded with his symbiont.

Initiation, Whispy sent. *What is the nature of the enemy?*

No enemy, James thought. *Just didn't want to get burned while I save someone trapped in a car.*

Little tactical value will be gained in non-combat scenarios with existing adaptations. Whispy huffed, his irritation pricking at James' mind.

Yeah, whatever. Someday you'll need to accept that I don't kick ass twenty-four/seven anymore.

Alternative suggestion: Recommend recovery of wounded from more extreme environments.

James threw open his door and sprinted toward the burning vehicle. The fire grew in those precious seconds, and the earlier would-be rescuers stumbled back, panicked looks on their faces. One man shouted into his cell phone. A few other people had gathered in the area, murmuring amongst themselves, everyone looking at the fire with concern.

The earlier Good Samaritans propped the injured truck driver against the side of a car. "My tire blew," he complained. "It's not my fault."

James ignored the crowd and the driver as he continued toward the burning SUV. He entered the outer ring of fire. The hungry flames licked at him, burning away patches of his clothes, but he barely registered a sting.

I wonder if I could march into hell with you and kick the Devil's ass, Saint Michael style?

Tactical abilities of the Devil entity are unknown at this time and irrelevant to immediate situation, Whispy replied. *Maximum adaptation already achieved against damage type,* he complained. *Restating: minimal tactical value of engagement.*

They'd been full partners for years, and even though the symbiont had become less robotic in many ways, Whispy had never embraced anything approaching James' fundamental morals and beliefs. He would have worried more, but the symbiont always did what he needed when he needed it to, and it wasn't like some other Vax was going to show up and take him. As far as the symbiont was concerned, the best way to continue becoming stronger was to serve James Brownstone. He just would never make the mistake of forgetting that Whispy Doom was fundamentally a weapon and always would be.

"That guy's going right into the fire!" someone shouted. "It's too hot, pal. I know what you're thinking, but you're just going to get yourself killed. It won't do you any good. Come back."

"That's not just some guy," a woman replied. She pointed. "That's James Brownstone."

Visible hope radiated from the faces of gathered people, and several clapped. A couple of people had had their phones out before, but now almost everyone pulled theirs out to start filming. No one could risk missing out on their piece of local history.

James groaned. It'd taken forever for all the media attention to die down after the incident with Nadina. For a while, every stupid day, some idiot reporter would call him or show up at the restaurant for "just a few questions about Colorado." It was hard to keep his life simple when reporters were constantly bothering him about shit that happened to incidentally involve him.

He shook his head and continued through the flames. This wasn't the time to bitch or worry. This was time to save a man's life. Whispy might not understand the value, but James didn't want to go to church and tell a priest that he had sat there and let a man die when he had a chance to save him. Kicking ass and barbeque were his normal contributions to society, but they weren't the only ones.

James arrived at the crumpled SUV. He grabbed the handle of the half-crushed door and pulled, but it didn't budge. He jammed his fingers into the cracks in the side and grunted as he yanked again. The metal buckled, but the door stayed in place. Being stronger than a normal man didn't mean being strong enough for every task.

The driver was the sole occupant of the smoke-filled vehicle. Blood covered his face, but his chest rose and fell. Smashing the window and pulling him out through the front might kill him. The flames might barely sting James, but the unconscious man inside didn't have that protection, and James didn't have a good way to extend it to him.

The fires had burned away half of James' pant legs, turning them into questionable jeans shorts, but he still had his pockets. He reached into a pocket and pulled out a small golden twig, a Shay treat. He placed it against the amulet.

Drain it, James ordered.

Alternate power source drained, Whispy sent. *Sufficient power for advanced transformation.*

I don't need most of that shit. Just need some armor on my legs and enough for the blade.

Silver-green tendrils spread over James' right arm and the bottom of his body; his pants were now mostly a collection of singed threads. He extended a blade and punched through the metal as if it were a thin sheet of paper and carved along the door until it fell off the SUV. Acrid smoke billowed out. He coughed.

Initiate alternate oxygen exchange or breathing modifications? Whispy asked

No. It's fine. We're done here.

A quick slice freed the man from the seatbelt, and James retracted the weapon. He pulled the man out, hefting him over his shoulder as he rushed out of the flames and smoke. He headed toward the gathered crowd, his armor preserving the modesty of his lower half. Most of his shirt remained, but a charred hole in the center revealed the bonded amulet and the tendrils extending into his chest. He'd long since stopped caring about people seeing the amulet. Everyone believed it was a magic artifact, and the few who knew the truth, even those who didn't fully trust him, had their own reasons to keep that secret. The Earth, they presumed, wasn't ready to know about the rest of the galaxy.

The crowd greeted James with cheers as he set the man down and examined him. James gritted his teeth. The man was no longer breathing. Besides the huge and deep laceration in his head, burns covered his body, and his legs were obviously broken. Had he taken too long?

"Shit," James muttered and checked the highway. Red-blue lights shone in the far distance, with only the faintest hint of sirens. Help was coming, but that didn't guarantee there were any ambulances with the first wave of responders. "This guy needs help," he bellowed. "Right now!"

"Is there a doctor around?" a woman called. "Or anyone who knows healing magic? Please!"

Everyone exchanged looks, desperation on their faces. A few people hung their heads in shame over their inability to help.

"Can't you do anything?" a man asked James, his expression pleading. He gestured toward the amulet. "Can you make it do a healing spell?"

"I can't do magic that way," James rumbled. "I just use things. This doesn't heal other people."

Please note alternative power liquid healing solution is still available, Whispy reminded him.

Shit. You're right.

James reached toward where his pocket would have been. The armor parted, and tendrils extended a small vial, one of two. The other was formulated for his specific needs, but he always kept one on hand for normal humans in case he was on an agency job and one of the bounty hunters was injured.

He grabbed the first potion from the tendril. "But this does heal other people." He raised the man's head, opened his mouth, and dumped the potion down his throat. If the victim was already dead, it wouldn't do any good.

I wonder if this shit will ever get cheap enough that everyone will carry it around? James thought. *We won't even need ambulances then. What good is all this magic garbage if people are dying in traffic accidents?*

Everyone stared at the SUV driver with pensive expressions, their breaths held. The seconds ticked by as the sirens grew closer.

Come on, James thought. *I just wasted a lot of money on you, so the least you can do is stay alive, so Shay won't give me shit later.*

The man gasped, and his eyes fluttered open. His burns began to fade as the gashes in his flesh knitted closed. The crowd exploded in raucous cheers, and a few people exchanged hugs.

The truck driver offered James a weak smile. "Do you have another one?"

"Sorry." James shrugged. "That was the only one that works on...humans." They could assume he was carrying Oriceran first aid. Highway Patrol cars and an ambulance zoomed down the road toward the accident. "But help's coming. You breathing all right?"

The injured truck driver nodded. "This shit hurts like hell, but I can still breathe."

The SUV driver sat up, blinking. "What happened?" He stared at his burning car and then at James. "Did you pull me out of there?" Wonder filled his voice.

"Dude," a light-haired young man nearby shouted. "Brownstone pulled you out of there by himself, and then he gave you a magic potion to save your ass. It's, like, straight-up superhero stuff."

James groaned. "It's not *superhero* shit. I just happened to be driving by. If there was a witch, elf, or gnome or someone like that nearby, they would have been able to save him easier than I did."

He wasn't a superhero. At least Alison could fly. He couldn't even pull that off in full Forerunner mode.

"I-I don't know what to say, Mr. Brownstone," the SUV driver stammered. "I'll let everyone know about what happened. I'll make sure they're shouting about it on the news."

James scrubbed a hand down his face. "Well, shit. So much for not having to deal with dumbass reporters."

CHAPTER TWO

J ames pulled his phone away from his ear and glared at it. It wasn't a video chat, but he hoped the reporter could sense his irritation before he lost control and did something he regretted, such as destroy his phone. This was doubly hard with his wife watching. He stood in front of the couch in his living room. Shay sat on the other end, watching him with a slight smirk, and Thomas lay curled up in his recliner, half-asleep. He was glad his loyal dog would live long enough to witness the birth of his child, but that thought only dampened his existing anger.

You would think these people would have bought a fucking clue after all these years, but the cycle starts over.

"No," James growled into the phone. "How many times do I have to tell you people that I'm not interested in this shit? Any of it. I don't care if it's a big, specially advertised exclusive, or you have some big payment you're going to give me for a few words on the record. I don't care what celebrity reporter you plan to send to interview me. I'm not interested. Is that clear? You could drive up to my house with a truck of the best barbeque ever made, and I still wouldn't be interested. If you know anything about me, then you should know if that wouldn't motivate me, you don't have a chance in hell."

"Mr. Brownstone, please be reasonable. This is a matter of public interest." The reporter sighed. "And I'm not asking for an exclusive. I'm just asking for a few comments on the record about what happened on the highway. This could be beneficial to you. I understand you value your privacy, but you acted, and now people are talking about it. You might as well take advantage of it, especially since you obviously haven't considered all the implications."

"What the fuck are you talking about? What implications?"

"You should keep in mind that your non-barbeque reputation is primarily associated with violence," the reporter explained, "whether some might consider it appropriate or not, such as the incident with Nadina. It couldn't hurt to highlight you using your abilities in a non-violent manner to save someone. Not only that, but you could share a few other pieces of information about your life. A lot of people are very interested. I understand that you're a private man, but a few comments, or even a short interview, would sate people's interest. It'll result in less trouble for you in the long run if you think about it, and it could drum up more business for your restaurant."

"I don't need advertising for my restaurant. I've got plenty of customers." His aggravation at the caller caused the words to come out in a half-growl. He doubted giving any small piece of information would satisfy people. In his experience, hungry people gobbled down more once they got a taste of something they liked. "What sort of comments are you even interested in, if not stuff about the accident?"

Years ago, he'd consider hiring a PR agent, but he had decided having one would, in and of itself, attract additional media attention by sending a signal that he wanted people to contact him about pointless interviews or sponsorships. He didn't need money and he didn't give a shit about fame, and he didn't understand why people wouldn't believe that despite him telling them over and over and over. Maybe he should get someone to take him to the moon, so he could carve the message into it.

"A lot of people would like to know a little more about your child," the reporter responded, hope in his voice. "There are so many mysteries there, and I don't think you understand how much the public craves knowledge about the first biological child of *the* James Brownstone."

"Whatever."

"Think about what a family profile could do for you, one you authorize rather than some unofficial thing. You could control the narrative a lot more than has happened in the past, especially with your adopted daughter. I understand why you hold some bitterness, but understand, Mr. Brownstone, that you could get the press working for you, rather than against you if you simply cooperated a little more."

Alison had experimented with cultivating a few reporter contacts to manage some of the press, and she had said it wasn't totally a miserable experience, but she'd always been better with people than him. If he tried something similar, it would end poorly.

James' hand tightened around his phone, but he stopped himself from squeezing any harder. He didn't need Shay mocking him for breaking another phone. He couldn't help it if they were so easy to snap. "I want to make this very clear," he began, his voice low. "I need you to listen, and to understand where I'm coming from."

"Yes, Mr. Brownstone? I'm more than happy to listen to anything you have to say. You can set the scope of our conversation. I might ask you a few things, but if you don't want to answer them, I understand. I won't try to force you to offer more information than you're comfortable with."

James resisted the urge to hurl his phone across the room.

None of these assholes ever gets it, no matter how many times I tell them. It's like I'm cursed.

"I won't be doing any fucking interviews," he explained. "I didn't save that man on the highway because I wanted reporters sniffing my ass. And before anyone even *thinks* about poking their damned nose into my family's life, they should ask themselves one important question because that's the only question they need to ask."

The reporter audibly swallowed. "A-and what question is that?"

"Are there any Harriken still around?" James rumbled. His jaw tightened, and he ground his back teeth. He let the question linger in the air, the implications clear.

"You can't possibly be implying what I think you're implying," the reporter sputtered. "I-I… Those people were criminals who hurt people. I'm not talking about doing anything unpleasant. I'm trying to help you, Mr. Brownstone. Everything I'm suggesting will help you."

"You want me to tell you something?"

"Yes, I do."

"Then I got something for you. 'No fucking comment.' And don't call me again." James killed the call and threw his phone on the couch with a loud growl.

Thomas raised his head to stare at the phone before dropping it again. The dog embodied the KISS philosophy better than his master and had long since learned to ignore it when said master became angry at the tiny metal slab. Of course, it was easier for a pet. It was not like he had reporters asking for his views on annoying neighborhood cats and birds.

James dropped onto the couch, his fists clenched. "That's the eighth fucking one today, and they've been swarming the restaurant like fucking vultures." He picked up his phone and turned it off. "Motherfuckers. At least the ones at the restaurant order something."

Shay laughed. "Vultures are carrion-eaters. Are you saying you're dead? I think I would have noticed, even with how sleepy I've been lately." She patted his shoulder.

He took a deep breath and slowly let it out. "I had all this shit nice and balanced. Why can't they leave us alone? There's always some new guy who thinks I'm going to open up to him and tell him all my secrets. Why can't they talk to someone else about this and buy a clue?"

"No good deed goes unpunished." Shay ran a hand over her swollen belly. "But threatening to murder reporters will probably not get them to leave you alone. They'll just write about what a dangerous and unstable man you are, and how the government needs to do something about you."

James snorted. "Half the government wishes they could send me to the World in Between, and the other half wants to keep me around in case they need someone to wrestle a giant space squid or some shit. Fuck reporters. Fuck the government."

Shay looked to the side and chuckled. "I don't care about the reporters, though. It's more what you did earlier that I think is funny."

"Earlier?"

She nodded. "You saving that man, and even going so far to use a healing potion on him."

"What do you mean?" James looked her way. "What's so funny about it?"

"When we met, you didn't do shit if you didn't get a paycheck." Shay pointed at him. "The only reason you even helped Alison at first was that she helped you, and you don't like being in anyone's debt. If some dragon was burning up half of Wyoming, you wouldn't have given a shit until the bounty came in. 'Not my fucking problem if they don't have dragon insurance.'" She related the last sentence in her best attempt at the low, rumbling voice of her husband.

James frowned. "I was a bounty hunter. I hunted bounties. It's in the fucking name. Nothing weird about that."

Shay rolled her eyes. "You're still technically a licensed bounty hunter, and you do all sorts of things to help people without worrying about bounties. I like how you tried to pretend that Nadina thing was inspired partially by bounties, but you wouldn't have cared. You would have looked into it all for free."

James growled. "That's different. That was about

barbeque. I'll always defend myself, my family, my friends, and barbeque for free."

His wife's look suggested she doubted that. "Oh? So if the Vax had shown up and said, 'We're just going to blow up Canada and leave,' you would have shrugged and said, 'Fuck it. There's no bounty, and I've got no close friends in Canada.'"

"The Canadian government would have issued a bounty, even retroactively." James snorted. "There's no way they wouldn't have."

"Maybe." Shay laid her head back on the couch. "But look at you now, running around saving random people's lives like you're a superhero."

"I'm not a fucking superhero," James complained. "People need to stop saying that shit."

Shay grinned as she looked at the ceiling. "I don't know. I've been saying for years that I've been fucking Superman. Accepting a little praise doesn't mean people are going to expect you to solve all their problems."

James wasn't as convinced of that. He groaned. "I didn't have a choice but to help the guy. That shit happened right in front of me. It's not like I'm purposefully driving around town trying to save random people for free and getting involved in stuff."

"Sure. Just keep pretending you're the stone-cold mercenary bounty hunter from when we first met." Shay waved a hand. "Whatever gets you through the day."

He grunted, not having a good response.

"There's nothing wrong with it," Shay added. "I think you should just accept that you're not the same man you were. It's been a lot of years and a lot of bodies, but people change." She lifted her head, her smirk even wider than before. "And before you say anything, I fully admit I'm nowhere near the same woman I was when I first met you, let alone when I faked my death. I only got a few years in with Alison, and motherhood is really going to keep my reflexive killing down—assuming no one screws with our kid. If they do that, they brought it on themselves."

James rubbed his temples. "I just don't want shit to get complicated again. We've got the kid coming, and he or she will take all our attention." He shrugged. "The agency's good. The restaurant's good. Everything is perfect, and we don't need reporters running around hassling us and messing with our perfect lives because they think they can use us to push their careers. Fuck them. If scaring them a little gets them off our backs, I'll do it.

"You do realize that you never getting attention is impossible, don't you? You might as well hope people vote you King of America and then issue a royal privacy decree."

"Why the fuck is it impossible? I've gotten the reporters off my ass before. If it happened before, it could happen again."

"I'm just saying, it'll always be temporary, no matter what you do or say." Shay snorted. "Because you're James Brownstone. No matter how hard you try, you're going to get involved in something that's a big deal because of who and what you are. The Vax might never come back, but they're hardly the only threat to the planet or the country, and at some point, you'll get dragged in because sometimes you just need a guy in alien armor to chop an asshole in half or blast them with a death ray."

"I'm not the fucking Army," James retorted. "It's not my responsibility to protect everyone and everything."

"No, but you *are* a one-man army," Shay observed. "And it's obvious now that you're aging slower than a normal human, so that means you might be around for a long time, leaving plenty of time for trouble to happen. The cold, hard truth is, you're never going to have true peace unless you retire and move deep in the mountains or to a hidden island on Oriceran or some shit like that. Unless you just want to give barbeque to bears, you might as well accept that you'll have to deal with reporters and other annoying assholes every three to six months." She nodded. "That seems about right."

"The mountains wouldn't be so bad," James muttered. "At least the bears would appreciate the damned food more than some of these bastards."

"Maybe Alison should think about it, too," Shay added, a concerned look on her face and the humor gone from her voice.

James frowned. "What do you mean? You think Alison should move to the mountains? She's better at handling this kind of attention, and she's got that English chick helping her."

"No. It's just like…" Shay sighed and held up her palms about a foot apart. "Imagine there's some sort of universal Brownstone Trouble Level set by God, the Devil, scheming super-intelligent magical dinosaurs, or whoever."

"Huh?" James had lost track of the conversation, and his attempts to figure out where it had gone only deepened his confusion.

"Just try to keep up."

James stared at her. "Trust me, I'm trying."

"It used to be that the amount of trouble you got into was more than her, kind of, but now you get in less trouble, and she gets in more." Shay pushed her hands together before moving back to the original distance. "But the universe demands a certain amount of Brownstone trouble no matter what, so it's got to go somewhere."

"What are you saying?" James furrowed his brow in confusion.

"I'm saying that you get in less trouble, but she gets in more." Shay shrugged. "It's not like I believe there's really some absolute Brownstone Trouble Level that must be satisfied. It's just a metaphor, and I get that a lot of that is because she's running that security company, but I just worry sometimes, is all. And it *feels* that way. That shit with the Tapestry was next-level weird, and I also don't like that she needed to get help from *those* other secretive assholes."

"Yeah, I get that. I don't know if I trust them fully either, but I'm surprised. I thought I was the one worrying too much about Alison. You were the one who was always telling me to sit down, shut up, and trust her. Why the change?"

"Yeah, I *have* been the one saying that. I'll admit that." Shay let out a quiet sigh. "The pregnancy's got me worrying more about our existing kid, even if she is an adult Drow princess who can blow up a building. I wish we could do more for Alison, with all the weird billionaires and other Drow princesses screwing with her. We're semi-retired from loud shit, and she's fighting giant monsters half the time. I get that she's got her own personal army and her fiancé's got her back, but I still worry."

James nodded slowly as he thought about how much Alison had changed. When he'd met her, she'd been a blind girl with a unique ability, but she didn't have access to most of her magic. She'd been a scared teen worried about her mother and betrayed by her father. Now, she was mentioned on the news constantly. More often than he was, for that matter. She'd earned allies from Oriceran to secret government agencies. He could understand where Shay was coming from since Alison's career was a source of both pride and terror.

"Yeah," he rumbled. "She's handled it well, and she's got a solid crew. We did everything we could to prepare her to take care of herself, just like we will with the new kid, except this time, we'll be in there from the beginning, so there won't be a lot of catch up."

Shay leaned toward him, her eyes narrowed in suspicion. "If I know you, you've probably got some strange plan for a toddler-sized combat assault course."

"Not an assault course." James shrugged. "But you know, exercise is good for kids."

She chuckled. "Fine. You know what? You're probably half right. We'll figure something out. We will make damned sure that no one even dares to try to bully our kid, but I'm not sure how much I trust you with that sort of thing."

"Yeah, well, we can talk to Lily and Alison about their warehouse training and how safe it was," James replied.

Shay laughed and patted her belly. "We didn't do a half-bad job with Alison, so we might even do a good job with the new kid. If you're accepting that your little girl has grown up, I need to get with the program." She shook her head. "And I need to go ahead and plop out this kid. I'm getting sentimental and soft. Maybe I need to kill a few people while I'm breastfeeding to get my cred back."

"You can't do that," James complained.

"Oh?" Shay raised an eyebrow. "You're suddenly worried about me? Even pregnant, I can handle myself."

"Nah, not worried about you, just think if you're shooting people while breastfeeding, it might hurt the baby's ears."

Shay grinned. "Alison's sibling is going to have a lot to live up to."

CHAPTER THREE

James stuck his spatula under the thick slab of light-brown meat and flipped it. He wiped some sweat off his brow, since the sun was shining down on the cloudless June day. The basic grilling of a protein needed to precede full barbeque mastery, and the former was his goal for the day. He eyed a large cooler next to the grill.

Nadina sent him the cooler full of meat, all taken from some Oriceran animal she managed to import on a limited-use license. He couldn't begin to pronounce the name, and it didn't have an English equivalent, other than his friend's description.

I wonder if I should be eating shit I can't even pronounce. I've eaten a lot of grilled meat all over Earth, but at least I could get in the ballpark of saying the name. In the end, at least those animals were mostly not strange, except for some of that shit I had in Hong Kong. I wonder if they lied to me and actually imported it from Oriceran?

"Just think of it as a six-legged magic cow," Nadina had suggested. "The meat's a lot sweeter than beef, though.

Much, much sweeter. I don't know if you'll like it, but you asked me about different sorts of Oriceran meat, so this is an interesting one to try. It'll give you an idea of the range of flavors that is potentially available."

James didn't like the fact that the elf had giggled after she described it and insisted that he at least try it. Allegedly, it was very popular in a kingdom on Oriceran known for their heavy meat-eating. He was inclined to trust his fellow semi-carnivores.

He frowned at the magic-cow steak. Having an open mind about meat didn't automatically grant him the knowledge and experience to produce something that tasted good, and while Nadina might be a successful pitmaster, she didn't serve her magic cow at any of her places. Was that just a product of supply, or indicative of its acceptability to the average human palate? Maybe even *she* couldn't cook it well.

As the steak sizzled, a strange odor wafted off it, overly fruity and sweet and reminiscent of pineapple. Shallow grill marks adorned the meat and, based on what Nadina had told him, the even color indicated the grilling was done. He plated the steak on a nearby paper plate. He didn't want to risk some lingering Oriceran strangeness on anything more permanent.

Shit, he thought as he closed the grill, suddenly realizing the implications. He hoped the magic cow flavor didn't permeate the grill. It'd be weird if it always smelled like pineapple.

James shook his head, trying to force the thought out. He needed to expand his horizons, which meant he couldn't be close-minded, and he'd occasionally have to risk lingering fruit odors. Besides, Nadina might mess with him a little, but she would never do anything that would screw with his grilling equipment, personal or professional. She had too much pride as a pitmaster for that.

Even if she had, there was nothing he could do now about the magic-cow meat tainting his grill. If it came down to it, he'd call one of the magicals who worked for the agency and ask for their help. There had to be some wizard or witch spell that could save a corrupted grill. He would concentrate on tasting his steak.

James grabbed the plate and walked over to a wooden table that stood underneath his patio overhang. He set the plate next to a knife and fork he'd already placed there. There was no sauce bottle because he wasn't sure about the flavor profile, let alone what might work to enhance it. Cooking was chemistry, but James relied more on years of experience and instinct rather than detailed knowledge for successful experiments. Unfortunately, he had no experience or knowledge concerning six-legged magic cows.

This is me doing what I need to do. This is me stepping right into the new world in a big way, not just a few spices and shit. I'm gonna expand into true pitmaster status, starting with magic cow.

James took a few deep breaths, then sliced a piece off and stabbed it with his fork, lifting it slowly, as if it might grow legs and attack him. With magic, a man never knew what was going to happen, and he didn't want to have to start wandering around with Whispy bonded just to try new proteins. The fork drifted closer to his mouth, the sweet scent growing almost overwhelming.

I should have asked her what it was supposed to smell like. For all I know, the shipping company screwed up, and it's rotten.

James plopped the meat in his mouth and chewed slowly. He grimaced and only didn't spit out the meat because he didn't want to disrespect Nadina. For all he knew, she was watching him with magic. The texture was strange; it was far smoother than he would have expected from the appearance, not completely unenjoyable but unexpected. A great flavor *might* have saved the steak.

Maybe an elf would argue the meat tasted delicious, but there was at least one man on Earth who would now argue the opposite to his grave. The bite started out sweet, the intensity of the flavor growing until his mouth and every part of his tongue were overwhelmed. It was as if someone had stuck a funnel into his mouth and poured in a pineapple smoothie mixed with blueberry cotton candy. No, even that combination would have been less sweet than what he was tasting. The sickening taste combined with the odd texture was too much. He shuddered and swallowed, praying for relief.

Was the fucking magic cow made out of sugar? Was Nadina just fucking with me? She had to know there was no way I would ever enjoy that.

James growled.

At least she can't say I didn't try it. Maybe I screwed it up, and I released all that sweetness because I didn't use the right temp. I'll have to ask her, but there's no way I'm offering that in my barbeque place. Even if it was milder than that, none of my customers would touch it.

James shook his head, the unpleasant flavor lingering in his mouth. He hadn't thought to prepare an emergency beer or glass of water. The new kid needed to be born and learn to walk so he could fetch him drinks when he needed them. His dog was too old to do much anymore except sleep or go on short walks around the neighborhood.

Shay slid the patio door open and stepped outside gingerly. "Oof. The doc keeps telling me the kid's a normal size, but I swear it's like having a bowling ball in here." She jabbed her finger at him. "This is your fault, you know."

"Kind of takes two to make a baby." James shrugged. "At least for humans. Probably not for every Oriceran."

"True. And it's not like I didn't enjoy the process." Shay sat on the edge of the table. "I just got off the phone with Alison."

His heart stayed steady. He needed to trust his daughter, especially after the conversation he'd previously had with Shay.

Is there trouble? It sounded like she was taking it easy the last time we talked. Only simple jobs, and the Drow princesses were training with her but not harassing her otherwise.

Shay's easy smile suggested no annoying conversations or revelations of new, dangerous organizations occurred during the call. James hoped so, but he would always have time to go kick ass for his first kid, even if she didn't need much help. For all her power and success, she was still his daughter, and he would always be her father.

His wife gestured to his plate. "Before we discuss her, I'm curious. How's your space cow?"

"It's not a space cow," James corrected. "It's a magic cow."

Shay snickered. "I stand corrected. And the flavor? Is it, you know, magically delicious?"

James grimaced, both at the joke and the memory of his sample. "It's awful. It tastes like a fruit cart exploded in my mouth. I'd rather have tofu turkey, and you know I feel about that abomination."

Shay raised an eyebrow. "I remember you threatened to throw the last guy who offered you some tofu turkey into the ocean, but I can see a market for people who might like your magic non-space cow."

"There will always be people who eat weird shit, but I'm not one of them." James pushed his plate toward her. "You want to try some?"

"That's okay, I'll live. And there's no way I'm trying it while I'm pregnant. For all I know, magic non-space-cow meat gives babies horns." Shay patted her pants pocket. "I mostly came out to tell you about Alison's call."

"What about her? She figure out her wedding shit yet?"

"Nope. She's still thinking about a lot of that, but our girl's going on an actual lengthy vacation. She's going to take a few weeks off here in about a week or so." Shay's smile grew warmer. "And she's going off the grid a little. There's some island she'll be visiting. It's run by magicals, but it's on Earth. Not that one with the Nereids. This place is an actual vacation spot. It sounds interesting, but I know you would hate it, and considering you hate all modes of transportation that aren't Ford trucks, you would bitch about going there." She rubbed her stomach. "Not that we're going on vacation for a while anyway. We'll consider it probably about the time you start the baby on the toddler assault course."

"When is she going?" James asked, imagining some strange Willy-Wonka-like magical island overrun by gnomes using spells that gave them green hair and orange skin. It was probably more mundane than that, given what he had seen from magicals over the decades, but the image stuck, and he chuckled.

"She's supposed to leave in the next few days," Shay explained. "But she should be back before my due date."

"Really? I'm surprised she's considering going, since we're so close now." James let disappointment creep into his voice. He liked the idea of his first child being there to greet his second.

Shay stared at him for a moment before her mouth quirked into a grin. "I'm glad I talked to her first. Very glad. This could have been a big mess."

James frowned. "What's that supposed to mean?"

"It means she was on the fence about even going. She was feeling guilty and said she would wait a few months, until after the birth. Until everything had settled down for us. I told her it's not like we can't handle our own kid, and if she wanted to help me, she should go on the damned vacation, so I don't have to worry about her overworking herself and being stressed out." Shay shook her head. "After dealing with those Tapestry freaks, Alison needs some time off. She doesn't know how to relax." She grinned at James. "She reminds me of how a certain stubborn man used to be. And sometimes still is."

He grunted. "I relax all the time. I was grilling just now. Sure, the meat was weird, but it's not like I'm hunting bounties or even working at the restaurant, and I find working at the restaurant relaxing. Except when a customer bitches. Or the grill breaks down. Or there's a vendor problem.

"Yeah, that sounds very relaxing."

James shrugged. "Even if that's true, I wouldn't have told her she shouldn't go on vacation. I don't want her to burn out."

"Good." Shay folded her arms. "I'm very glad to hear that we're in agreement. Besides, even if something were to happen, I don't need my daughter at my side during the birth. I need my husband. Keep that in mind."

"I'm not going anywhere." James shrugged. "I haven't even left the county in a while."

"I'm just saying no road trips for a while, probably three or four months." Shay nodded, wearing a self-satisfied look on her face.

"I've got no reason to go on a road trip," James replied. He gestured to the plate. "I know I'm not going to pick up any more of the magic cow soon. I can talk to Nadina about trying out different Oriceran meats and having her ship them to me. She's got a better handle on the import process anyway."

Shay's smile faded to a look of concern. "There's another thing. It might not be a real issue, but ignoring shit isn't usually a good idea for people with our unique backgrounds." She averted her eyes.

James narrowed his eyes. "What are you talking about? Is anything wrong?"

Shay took a deep breath and slowly like out. "I was checking something the other day, and I was wondering if you might have a clue about it." She pulled out her phone, and after some tapping, slid it over to her husband. "I thought I saw the same green car a few times the other day, but I didn't recognize it from the neighborhood. So I pulled some footage from our cameras. It turns out the same car has passed us several times in the last few days."

"You have made a point of memorizing all the neighborhood cars? I didn't know that."

Shay nodded. "Just because I'm not one-hundred-percent paranoid anymore, it doesn't mean I'm not ninety-percent paranoid."

James' stomach tightened. He didn't want to believe anyone was idiotic enough to target his house and his pregnant wife, but maybe he'd miscalculated. Shay, even pregnant, could take on most people who might want to mess with her, but she would damned well avoid it if he had any say. First, he needed to establish what was actually happening.

"Maybe they're friends of someone in the area," he suggested, trying to push the worry down. "It's not like we live on a dead-end street or a cul de sac."

"I thought of that, but there's one thing that makes me wonder." Shay shook her head. "They always slow down when they pass our place. Maybe they're just fans, but given how many times they've come by in the last few days, it might be a stalker."

"Why didn't you tell me before?" James asked, his gaze dipping to her belly. "If there's a threat to the baby, we need to handle it as soon as possible."

"I've been moody and emotional lately," Shay replied. "I thought I might have just been seeing things. Paranoid. Well, more paranoid than usual." She shrugged. "If I freaked out and cried to you every time I've been extra-suspicious since getting pregnant, we'd be investigating half of Los Angeles, and probably blowing up a third of it."

James peered at the car's image. It was a dark green Honda, non-electric judging by the tailpipe. Numerous dents and rust marred the vehicle. He wasn't an expert on any vehicle other than Ford trucks, but it was obvious the car was closer to the era of his F-350 than the average vehicle on the road these days.

"Not exactly some high-end assassin if they're driving shit like that," James rumbled.

"Yeah, and I doubt they would be so damned obvious." Shay snickered. "I'm not saying they are a high-end assassin. Too much window tint to get a good visual on the driver, but the car is registered to a Calista Everton. From what I can tell, she's a college student. Started attending UCLA last fall, but I didn't do a deep dive, and I didn't want to mess around too much at the college. Don't shit where you live or work, you know?"

What the fuck? It can't be.

"Calista?" James murmured. "Why is Calista coming by our place?"

Shay blinked. "Wait. You know her?"

"Yeah. She lived at the orphanage the last few years until she was eighteen, originally came there when she was fourteen. Had a real rough time, but they helped her turn things around. She still volunteers there sometimes, but, yeah, last I heard, she'd started college. She's a quiet girl, but I haven't talked to her much lately or even before. No more than a lot of the kids there, and I've barely seen her over the last few months." James searched his memories, trying to find anything that would explain why Calista would be in his neighborhood or near his house.

Shay sighed. "You'd better check on her, James. It might

be a coincidence, but there are only so many coincidences I'll believe when it comes to you."

"She's not a magical," James replied.

"And you sure this girl isn't in love with you?"

James groaned. "She didn't act like it. She's just a normal girl. She wouldn't be mixed up in any strange trouble."

Shay gave him a pitying look. "I'm not a magical, and I killed my first man when I was younger than her. And you were an alien when you were that age and didn't even know it. Just give her a call. Maybe there's a perfectly innocent explanation."

James let out a little grunt. "I'll call her in a little bit. I'm sure this shit is nothing."

"I hope so, for her sake."

CHAPTER FOUR

James stared at his phone as he sat on the edge of his bed. A quick call to Charlyce, who still volunteered several days a week at the orphanage, had gotten him Calista's number. Charlyce didn't even ask why he needed it; she'd spent enough years working for him at the agency to understand that sometimes it was best not to ask too many questions when James Brownstone asked a favor. The incident didn't warrant him calling in an infomancer or other official agency resources. It wasn't like he needed an entire team to look into one teenage college girl acting strangely.

What do I do if she is a stalker? I can't threaten someone from the orphanage, and I don't want to get the cops involved if I don't have to. Fuck. First things first; better make sure this shit actually is something and not just Shay being paranoid.

He dialed and waited, staring at his faded bedroom wall. They needed to paint it, but the idea sounded annoying. Maybe there was some artifact Shay had in the warehouse that would automatically paint his wall. He could always pay a magical. It'd be ridiculously expensive compared to hiring someone to come and paint it, but he wouldn't have to be inconvenienced. He refused to ask one of the magicals at the agency to do that kind of thing. It didn't feel right.

"Hello?" Calista answered, breaking him out of his painting thoughts. "Is this…Mr. Brownstone? The caller ID says so, but I'm having trouble believing it. You've never called me before."

"Yeah," James rumbled. "It's me. I don't think anyone would be dumb enough to try to fake being me." He scoffed. "If they did, they'd last about as long as the Widowmaker did after pretending to be Shay."

"The Widowmaker?" Calista sounded confused. "Who is the Widowmaker?"

"Don't worry about it. That was a long time ago, and she's dead."

"O-okay," Calista replied. "It definitely sounds like you. But why are you calling, Mr. Brownstone? I don't think I've talked to you in a long time. I've seen you at church now and again, but it's not like you're chatty there with anyone other than the priests. I vaguely remember saying, like, a couple of words to you at the orphanage a few months ago, but I don't even remember what the conversation was about."

Is it just me, or is she trying too hard?

James might not be great at reading people, but he didn't need to be sensitive or magical to hear the obvious tension in her voice. He couldn't set aside the reality that people found him intimidating, and even if the orphans in recent years had gotten more used to his regular appearances, including Calista before her departure, dealing with him in that setting was different than getting a call out of nowhere from a class-six bounty hunter known for, as the reporter had mentioned, a history of violent encounters. Collateral damage was part of being in his world.

"I have something to ask you," he explained, trying his best to dampen his default voice, something approaching the love child of a growl, an earthquake, and a distant explosion. "It'll be quick, and then you don't have to talk to me for a long time."

"Oh, I almost forgot," Calista replied. "I've never had a chance to say congratulations about your wife getting pregnant. I've been trying to volunteer, but I just haven't had as much time to be at the orphanage this last year. It's not like you're there every day, and it just seemed weird to go up to you in church even after they announced it. I-I understand why you don't come to the orphanage all the time, but you know, congratulations. It's like the priests are always saying, children are a blessing and the future and all that."

She's definitely trying too hard to deflect. What the hell is she hiding?

"Let's cut the bullshit, Calista." James inhaled deeply through his nose and slowly let it out. "Are you in trouble?"

Her breath caught. "Trouble? Why you ask me something like that? I'm not in any trouble. My grades are excellent. My scholarship is fine. Did one of the priests ask you to call and check on me?"

"No, I don't mean that kind of trouble." James didn't want to admit he hadn't even thought of the possibility. "But if you aren't in trouble, why are you driving by my house so much?" He let the rumble return to his voice. He didn't want to scare the girl any more than she already was, but he couldn't help her if she wouldn't tell him the truth. A little push might be needed.

She had to understand one important truth about the world. There were a lot of frightening people in it, but none of them were scarier than James.

Is this really my business? It's not like she could threaten Shay or me on her best day, and it's not like she cared all that much about the visits at the orphanage. Why would she suddenly decide to stalk me?

"Your house?" Calista sighed. "I-I can explain."

Wait. Shit. There's one possibility. Damn it. Why didn't I think of it before?

"You're not a journalism major, are you?" James asked.

"No. I'm majoring in social work. Why did you think I was a journalism major?" Calista returned to sounding more confused than frightened. "I don't think I've ever even thought about that."

Okay. So she's not an intern of some vulture reporter.

"I've not… Oh." Calista let out a strangled laugh. "I get it now. It took me a while, but I realized I needed to think like a bounty hunter, even if you don't do that stuff as much anymore. The driving by your house…is that the main reason you're calling?"

"Yeah," James replied. "You could say that."

"You're misunderstanding the situation, Mr. Brown-stone. There is someone I've been meeting in your neighborhood. It's got nothing to do with you. It's a complete coincidence."

"Meeting someone in my neighborhood?" James asked,

his voice laced with incredulity. "Even though you slow down as you pass my house a lot of the times?"

"Yes. For school." Calista sounded irritated. "It's not a crime to slow down on a street, Mr. Brownstone. I'm not trying to be a bitch about it, but listen to yourself."

"Who?" James asked.

"Who what?"

"Who are you meeting in the neighborhood?" James demanded. "I host a lot of neighborhood barbeques. I know everyone in this area, and half of them work for me. So, who are you meeting?"

"That's not really your business," Calista snapped. "Just because you donated to the orphanage doesn't mean I have to get your permission for how I live my life. Back off."

You think you can blow me off that easily? Try again, girl.

"What was the meeting about?" James pressed. "Social work?"

"You know what? This is turning weird. You're acting like a stalker. I'm done with this. I appreciate what you did for the orphanage, and I always will, but don't ever call me again, okay?" Calista killed the call.

James tossed his phone on the bed and grunted. Poking his nose into someone else's business when they didn't ask for help seemed like a good way to prove Shay right about how much he had changed. He had no concrete proof Calista *wasn't* meeting someone in his neighborhood, other than the fear in her voice and her slowing down. Could she have been scared of him? Maybe she was taking selfies to impress friends at school. The orphans knew how much he abhorred media attention, so she might have thought he would be offended by her actions.

That explanation didn't sit well with him. None of the kids at the orphanage had ever seemed scared of him. The last few times he'd dealt with Calista, she had been happy. She'd talked to him about what it felt like to go into the larger world, despite having a rough life. He could relate to that, just like everyone who had grown up at the orphanage.

I should leave this shit alone. I'm no superhero. It's not my job to save every random-ass person in this city. I'm just a man with a new kid on the way who likes barbeque and eats the occasional magic pineapple-tasting cow. This isn't a problem.

James groaned and scrubbed a hand over his face. There was one problem with his logic. She wasn't a random-ass person.

An hour later, James knocked lightly on an oak office door tucked in the back of his church.

If he tells me to back off, that'll be enough. At least I'll be able to let this go.

"Come in," Father Rojas called from inside.

Father McCartney, despite his good works, had grown frail with the advancing years. He had been focusing in recent years mostly on Mass and parish administration, and the bishop had recently assigned Father Rojas to the church to aid with community outreach efforts, including the orphanage. James' funding, combined with the efforts of dedicated volunteers, including Charlyce and former residents, ensured the current kids didn't lack for attention or help.

James didn't have anything against the younger priest, but he hadn't grown up around him either, so it'd been an awkward transition. Father McCartney was almost as much as a surrogate father as Father Thomas had been. No one liked to confront the mortality of their parents, biological or otherwise.

Father Rojas smiled and looked up from his desk. He gestured to the chair. "I wasn't expecting you today, James."

"Sorry." James sat on the offered seat. "This is probably stupid sh…" He took a few deep breaths. Being in church mandated more self-control than normal. For a brief period, he'd at least gotten out of the habit of cussing around Alison when she was younger, but that hadn't lasted long. Maybe he'd do better with his younger child. His lifestyle changes had led to fewer trips to Confession, where he had to explain away killing dozens of gangsters.

"Is there something troubling you?" Father Rojas threaded his fingers together and set his hands on his desk. "I understand if you're feeling a little nervous about your coming child. Children are a blessing, but that doesn't mean they aren't daunting. Feel free to visit me anytime to discuss this transition in your life. I've mentioned it to you before, but you're welcome to attend any of our classes on being a new parent."

James shook his head. "Nah, I already went through all that worrying about the kid stuff, and I'm fine. It was nothing a little barbeque couldn't solve. You can solve most things with barbeque."

"So I've heard you express many times." Father Rojas smiled. "Then what's troubling you? It's rare that you seek counsel outside the confessional."

"I don't always pay attention to people during Mass," James began with a nod in the general direction of the nave.

"I hope you're at least paying attention to the priests." Father Rojas laughed. "And you're paying attention enough to at least participate when necessary."

"Calista Everton," James clarified.

Father Rojas tilted his head, still smiling, but confusion playing across the rest of his face. "What about her, exactly?"

"Has she been acting strangely?" James asked.

Father Rojas's smile faded and was replaced by a slight frown. "What are you getting at?"

"I was just wondering if she's been acting strange." He tried to keep any hint of threat out of his voice. There were certain lines he wouldn't dare cross, especially in a church.

The priest leaned back in his seat and sighed. "I suppose that depends on how you define 'strange.'"

"Changes in her expected behavior, for one thing," James explained.

"She has not been coming to church as much," Father Rojas admitted. "But it's not like that's a surprise to any of us, with her starting college. It isn't unusual for young people making the transition to college. It usually levels out, and the faithful return to more regular attendance. I asked her if she's attending a church closer to the college, and she said no. She has to work extra hard as well, so that might play into it."

James frowned. "Why is that?"

"Because she has her own apartment." Father Rojas shrugged like the explanation told him everything.

"I don't get it. You expected her to have a house?" James' brow wrinkled in frustration. The priest might not purposely have been being cryptic, but the net result was the same.

Father Rojas chuckled. "I say this as a point of establishing a baseline and not to provide anything that might be perceived as an insult, James. But keep in mind you didn't go to college. Your calibration is off, in a sense."

James shrugged. "So what if I didn't go? My wife is a college professor, and my daughter went to college. It's not like I've never set foot on a college campus."

He resisted pointing out that his showdown with the Vax had occurred at a college. The government probably wouldn't appreciate him spilling a national security matter just to make a point to Father Rojas.

"Then let me be clear where I'm coming from." Father Rojas lowered his hands and set them in his lap. "Regardless of whether the domicile is a dorm, apartment, or house, for financial reasons, most college students live in shared settings unless they have external funding. Calista spent most of her teenage years in the orphanage. She worked hard in school and earned her scholarship, but as an adult, it's not like the church or the orphanage is providing her additional funds to live by herself. She's chosen to live in her own apartment, and while it isn't extravagant, it does mean she needs to earn a little more money on the side to be able to afford it. That's all I'm saying. We're trying to support her in this time of transition. She's had a solid first year at school."

"Why does she live by herself?" James asked. "Why not get a roommate?" He didn't see anything all that wrong with that situation, but additional insight into the reason might help him understand how and why she might be in trouble. The fact that she needed extra money already pointed to a number of disturbing possibilities. It wasn't like the average criminal would dare to screw with the orphanage or most people connected to him, but he doubted Calista went around advertising to everyone that she used to live at an orphanage mostly funded by James Brownstone.

"She lives by herself for the same reason I imagine you didn't want a roommate when you left the orphanage," Father Rojas replied. "After years of living in a crowded group setting, many of our former charges prefer their own space. It's understandable. They want to get to know themselves as individuals."

"Could she be having money problems?" James asked.

"She's been working a lot more since the summer started. My understanding is, her plan is to save up enough that she can work less during the fall semester." Father Rojas sighed. "James, what is this all about? Is Calista in some sort of trouble?"

"I don't know," James admitted. "My wife has seen her a few times in the neighborhood near our place, and when I called Calista to ask why, she sounded scared. It might be nothing, but it's hard for me to let sh...stuff like this go. Did she say anything in Confession?"

The priest's disapproving stare made James twitch. "Please, James. We all appreciate everything you've done for the orphanage, parish, city, and country, but Confession is sacred. Besides..." He looked down with an uncertain expression. "I haven't been serving as her confessor.

You could speak to another priest, but I'd strongly advise you not to do that. We both know Father McCartney wouldn't appreciate it." He raised his head, his face steely. "If this building has any meaning, it's because we respect the sacraments of our faith. If you think Calista's in trouble, then I encourage you to look into things. We'll do our best to reach out to her, but you must do it without asking any of us to violate the seal of the Confessional."

James grunted. "I understand. This might be nothing other than a moody college girl having trouble between semesters with a bad boss or something."

Father Rojas smiled. "I appreciate that you care enough to check into her. The parish couldn't ask for a better guardian."

Great. I'm locked into this. This better not be something stupid like she broke up with her boyfriend.

CHAPTER FIVE

James pulled off the street in front of the modest two-story apartment building. Peeling paint and a few cracks proved Calista's landlord needed to spend more money on maintenance, but James had kicked in the door of many shadier places in his career. There were no obvious criminals or suspicious men lingering in the neighborhood, which was filled with nearly identical apartment buildings. Bright streetlights illuminated the area. He could see the appeal for a young, single woman.

Shit. I'm the stalker now.

James stepped out of his truck and slammed the door. He wasn't sure if Calista was home, but another call to Charlyce netted him her general work hours. Calling ahead wasn't an option. He couldn't risk her running.

The stairs creaked under his heavy footfalls. As he crested the stairs, a man parted his blinds in a nearby apartment and grimaced. He then ducked, letting the blinds hide him.

James stared at the window. The apartment was two

down from Calista's, but being afraid of a large tattooed man wearing Resting Ass-kicking Face wasn't inherently suspicious. Not everyone wanted someone like him around, even if they didn't have a bounty. But if the man had been harassing Calista, a very loud conversation would be coming, one punctuated with a few new holes in the wall. James could always pay the landlord for the damage.

With an annoyed growl, James headed toward Calista's place. The blinds were drawn, and the lights were off.

Shit. She's not home. Or is she? I need to be smart about this.

He pulled out his phone and dialed her number.

Calista picked up after the fourth ring. "I-I thought I told you to never call me again, Mr. Brownstone," she answered, her voice quaking. "If I wasn't clear, then let me make sure you know now."

Is she really that afraid of me? Or is she afraid of someone else?

"Hey, I wanted to stop by and talk to you," James explained. "I'm at home," he lied. "So I wanted to make sure I didn't drive across town for no reason. When are you going to be home?"

"I'm at home now, but it doesn't matter. I'm going out of town for a few days, and I'm leaving in the next thirty minutes. Not only that, this is harassment. Everyone knows the cops won't stand up to you, but if you call again, I'm going to tell Father McCartney you're harassing me after I asked you to stop."

James glanced at her darkened windows. "I'm not harassing you. I think something's wrong. You don't hunt bounties for as long as I did without picking up when people might be in trouble or scared or something. I can

50

help you. I already talked to Father Rojas about this, and he said I should look into it, so it's not like I can walk away with a clean conscience."

Calista's laugh sounded hysterical. "Are you kidding me? You went and harassed Father Rojas? You're a crazy stalker. If you know what's good for you... Screw it. I've got to go. I'm changing my number tomorrow. Next time you contact me, I'm calling the cops." She ended the call.

James slipped his phone back into his coat. He stuck his hands in his pocket and waited for lights to turn on or the door to open.

Something's wrong. But what? That was fucking terror in her voice, and it's not because of me. I'd bet my restaurant on that. She's just a college kid, though, so what could she even be involved in? Maybe stupid drug shit?

I'm sure the cops won't mind if I loudly encourage a few dealers to leave town.

James cracked his knuckles before lightly knocking on the door. The unlocked door opened a few inches. He frowned. What kind of paranoid woman left her door unlocked?

Maybe she's just lazy.

He knocked again and waited. No one called out or appeared in the next minute.

James pushed the door open. "Calista? You in here? It's James Brownstone. We've got to talk about this shit. I don't care if you think I'm not minding my business. I'm not a stalker. My wife put me up to this, and a man doesn't tell his pregnant wife she's being crazy if he wants to live until the next day."

He narrowed his eyes as he finished opening the door.

Shattered glass from broken picture frames littered the floor near the front door. The small flat-panel TV lay on the ground. The couch was spotted with holes ringed by charred, blackened fabric.

"Calista?" James bellowed, flipping on the light. A burned chair lay on its side, the floor untouched, which indicated magic had been used. Red-brown spots led from the kitchen. It didn't look like enough blood to be a fatal wound, but any suspicious blood in a trashed apartment wasn't a good sign.

He yanked out his gun and growled, "You in here? Because this shit doesn't look like you're okay."

The light whir of the air conditioning was his only answer.

Am I too fucking late? Damn it.

James crept into the kitchen, his gun at the ready. Unlike the living room, other than the tall stack of dishes in the sink, the room wasn't in disarray. His checks of the bathroom and bedroom revealed the same.

Calista wasn't there, and the specific nature of the damage in the living room suggested something far more dangerous than drug dealers. He tucked his gun back into the holster. The legally correct move would be to contact the police, but if he needed to deliver revenge later, involving them early on could complicate matters. Davion might be able to follow a trail, but the obvious signs of magic also meant even the infomancer might have trouble.

Should I let Father Rojas and Father McCartney know? Nah. Same shit. The less they know about anything I might do beforehand, the better it is for them.

The harsh buzz of James' phone snapped him out of his thoughts. To his surprise, the call was from Calista.

"Where the fuck are you?" James barked into the phone. "Your front door is open, and your living room is torn up. Don't try to tell me you're not in any fucking trouble."

Someone clucked their tongue on the other end. "Tut, tut, Mr. Brownstone," a man said in a cheerful tone. "Such inappropriate language to use when speaking to a young woman. You're such a crass individual. I know that, of course, but encountering it directly is revealing."

"Fuck that, and fuck you. Who are you, and where is Calista?"

"That isn't information you need at this time," the man responded, his voice still cheerful. "There's only one important fact that's relevant in this conversation, and that you should take under consideration. If anything, it's arguably the single most important relevant piece of information."

James took a deep breath. "And what's that, asshole?"

"You've already seen her apartment, which of course I know because I've been watching it. But you visiting makes this easy. You understand what I am, I trust? Barbeque hasn't rotted your brain?" The man chuckled.

"From where I stand, you're a fucking wizard with a death wish."

The man's chuckle turned into a hearty laugh. "The latter I could quibble with, but the important thing is my possession of magical abilities, which means I'm not some mere gangster you can push around with ease."

"I've killed plenty of wizards."

"Let me make this immediately clear," the wizard

answered. "If you call the police, by the time they find this girl, she will be in pieces and burned to a crisp."

James' loud snarl would have frightened off an entire pack of rabid wolves. "Do you understand who you're fucking with? Do you have any idea how many fuckers I've killed because they thought they could push me around? Even I don't, because I lost count of all those pieces of shit. You're just another number to me, asshole."

"You're quite the crude one, aren't you?" The man sighed. "Yes, I'm well aware of the kind of savage you are. I'm not an idiot, Mr. Brownstone. That's why I have a nice hostage now. I took your previous behavior into consideration."

Damn it. I need to throw him off the scent.

"What makes you think I give a fuck about that girl?" James asked.

"Oh, let's not attempt such feeble lies. If you didn't care about Miss Everton, you wouldn't be in her apartment after she so rudely tried to scare you off. It's not as if I think you have a deep relationship with her, but your involvement with that orphanage is hardly a state secret. The kind of man who attends his church faithfully and gives money to a church orphanage is also the sort of man who isn't going to leave one of his fellow parishioners and orphans in the hands of a nasty and homicidal wizard who likes to burn things. I'll be nice, though. I'll at least render her unconscious before I kill her. I'm not a total monster."

James lowered the phone and smashed his fist into Calista's coffee table. Splinters of wood shot from the table as the piece of furniture cracked in the middle and collapsed into two pieces.

"You can't win against me," he threatened, his voice low and infused with deadly promise. "I'm a man who has spent years finding all sorts of rogue magicals. I will fucking find you, and I will rip you apart. If you're not a total damned idiot, then I shouldn't need to list all the people I've put down throughout the years, and that's just the ones who were public knowledge. Do you understand, dipshit?"

"That's the thing about power, Mr. Brownstone," the man replied. If he was afraid at all, his happy voice didn't betray it. "It's only useful if you're willing and able to use it, and as long as I have this hostage, you won't. I've studied you extensively, so much so I could write a lovely biography. Even before your…domestication, you weren't a ruthless man willing to kill innocent people, let alone innocent young women. It's why you were drawn into the entire affair with the Harriken, after all. Arguably, the fact that there's an Alison *Brownstone* is proof of your weakness in regard to vulnerable young women."

James snorted. "And you think you can succeed where an entire group of gangsters couldn't? They had artifacts and hired magical hitmen."

"I've studied their mistakes, and I think I'm more prepared, so yes. This doesn't have to be a difficult situation, Mr. Brownstone, and it doesn't have to end with anyone getting hurt, provided you act in a reasonable manner. You can do that, can't you?"

"And what the fuck are you defining as 'a reasonable manner?'" James snapped. "Because right now, I'm thinking reasonable is breaking you into two pieces instead of five."

"You're a wealthy man," the cheerful wizard observed.

"You could be far wealthier, but your investments and bounties alone mean you could never work a day for the rest of your life and be fine. And given your modest appetites, a lot of that money is wasted on you."

James let out a dark chuckle. "What? You're trying to squeeze money from me? That's what this shit is?"

The man replied with a merry laugh. "I'm suggesting that all that money isn't being effectively utilized. What good is money if you don't spend it? You're not doing your part to stimulate the economy, whereas a man of less simple needs will spread it around more. So, I would suggest you go retrieve, let's say, two million in cash in a briefcase. You're going to get that money in the next twenty-four hours and drop it off at a location I'll pass along. If you don't, you can spend some of it on Miss Everton's funeral."

"I'm going to really enjoy killing you," James offered. "It's gonna be quick, though. That's not me being merciful. I just really, really want to kill you, and the killing's the important part, not the process."

"Oh, come now. Is your personal satisfaction more important than this young woman's life?"

James tightened his jaw. Without any clues to Calista's location, even if he had a portal, there was no way he could guarantee he could get there before the jolly bastard killed her.

"Why cash?" James asked. "Isn't that a little old-school? Too traceable? Why not TrollCoin or shit like that?"

The wizard scoffed. "Don't take me for the lackwits you're used to hunting. As I said, Mr. Brownstone, I've studied you extensively. I know your agency employs hackers and infomancers. Mundane criminals might think that cryptocurrencies will save them from you, but I know better. I've got the magic and artifacts to keep you from tracking that cash once I have it."

"Even *if* you get the cash from me, you're dead. You realize that? All I have to do is put out word to every organized crime group in this city that you fucked with me, and if I don't find you, they will. They'll make an example out of you, so I don't make an example out of them."

"Oh, how nasty of you." The wizard clucked his tongue again. "But I'll have two million dollars in addition to my existing funds, and it's not as if I need to stay in LA. I hear Chile's nice since you cleaned it up a while back, but I'll have the entire world. You can always say no. Turn me down. Be a tough guy. You're a religious man. Is it such a terrible thing for me to send an orphan girl to join her parents?"

James' nostrils flared. If the wizard had been in front of him, he would have already kicked him through a couple of walls and then snapped his neck.

"Put her on the phone," James ordered. "I need to make sure she's still alive. And let me be clear—if I get you your money and you try any shit, there's nowhere you can run on Earth or Oriceran where I won't find you. You said you know all about me?"

"Yes, I do," the man responded, smugness lacing his voice.

"Then you know the Drow Queen thought she could fuck with me, and you know what happened to her."

The wizard scoffed. "The Oriceran queen being surprised by you is one thing. I'm a fine and knowledgeable Earth native. I know how to hide from angry bounty hunters."

"Put her the fuck on the phone," James spat through gritted teeth. Mr. Jolly Wizard had earned himself a free death sooner or later, but saving Calista was the priority.

"I'm sorry," the girl sobbed. "I'm so sorry. I tried to warn you, but you just kept coming."

"What happened?" James asked, keeping his tone even. "How did you get mixed up with these guys?"

"I don't even know why they came to me." She sniffled. "They just showed up at my apartment last week and said they would give me a hundred thousand dollars to seduce you. I told them to screw off, and I was going to go tell you and the cops. They told me if I breathed a word to anyone, they'd kill me and Father Rojas and Father McCartney. They even threatened to burn down the orphanage. They gave me a time limit. I came by your house all those times, but I just couldn't bring myself to knock on your door. And then I—"

The sounds of her sobs grew distant as scratching came over the line.

James closed his eyes and sucked in a low, deep breath. His heart galloped in his chest, and his pulse pounded in his ears. It took all his self-control not to crush his phone, and he had no doubts that if he was bonded to Whispy, he would have more than enough power for extended advanced mode. Maybe even Forerunner. He didn't even realize he was growling for several seconds.

"It really is uncouth for a man of your wealth to sound like an animal," Mr. Jolly Wizard suggested over the line. "I wish the girl hadn't explained all that, but you see, it's really her fault for not taking my generous offer. She could have had all her financial worries go away, along with bragging rights to her friends about screwing you." He sighed, genuine disappointment in the sound. "Makes more sense to give it up to James Brownstone than some idiot college boy, right?"

"I…. Will. Kill. You," James slowly replied.

"Sure, sure. I'll live in terror all my days. In the meantime, twenty-four hours, Mr. Brownstone. Get the money and drop it off at the second closest table from the entrance at Amazing Dwayne's. When you leave the restaurant, you'll find the girl in the parking lot waiting for you." He rattled off the address. "There are several restaurants in LA, so make sure you're at that specific one. I know you forget nothing, so I won't insult you by telling you to write it down. You're familiar with Amazing Dwayne's, right?"

The blind rage cleared for a moment, and James' body trembled with anger. Amazing Dwayne's was a kid's pizza chain founded by a gnome five years prior. There were dozens all over California, and they had recently expanded into Nevada. They were famous for their singing magical automatons.

This fucker is going to put more kids at risk.

James hadn't wanted to kill someone this badly in many years. The average idiot he ran into was more an annoyance than truly rage-inducing. That was the main reason he'd been forced to carry Shay treats.

"Do we have a deal, Mr. Brownstone?" Mr. Jolly Wizard asked, mirth leaving his voice for the first time in the conversation. "If not, you can listen to her die right now over the phone. Two million dollars is a real bargain for a man of your means. See, I'm not greedy. I could have asked for ten times as much."

"We have a deal," James rumbled.

"Good. No cops. You know how this will end if you get them involved. This is just going to be a private deal between you and me. Not that they would help. Don't worry, this isn't personal. This is only about the money." The call ended.

No cops? Fine. I don't need cops for what I'm going to do to you.

CHAPTER SIX

James stared out of the front window of his truck. He'd spent far too much time imagining all the different ways he could destroy Mr. Jolly Wizard. Accidental arrogance born of ignorance was at least excusable, but this was a man who had gone after James and an innocent girl with careful planning and foresight. The wizard had no excuses for his actions, and James had no reason to grant him even the tiniest mercy.

It's like the accident was a sign. Just when I think every-thing's going okay, some fucker has to roll up and cause trouble. Can't blame me for taking the challenge.

It didn't matter how creative a punishment James devised if he couldn't find the kidnapper. That meant he would need good assistance in the form of particularly annoying but skilled help. He brought up his contacts and hit the number for Davion.

"Good evening, brah," the infomancer answered. "How's it hanging?" Although he was a jolly and cheerful wizard as well, James didn't want to kill him. At least not on most days. All his rage was targeted at Mr. Jolly Wizard anyway.

"I need your help," James replied. There was no reason to mess around. Although he had twenty-four hours, that might not be a lot of time to mount a rescue, depending on where the kidnapper was hiding.

"Righteous. You always have the best stuff for me to do, and not just hacking some douchebag bounty's phone. But I didn't think you were taking on any bounties for a while. That's what Maria said, anyway. She also said to leave you alone and not to piss you off until after the baby was born."

"This isn't a bounty. Not that I know of, but even if it is, I don't care." James clenched his jaw. "This is personal. This is a motherfucker who thinks they can spit in my face and threaten people, and that I'll just take it."

"Woah," Davion replied, wonder in his tone. "This sounds like Harriken-level disrespect, brah. Bust their shit up."

"Yeah, you could say that, and it's gonna end the same way." James grunted. "Maybe not blowing up an entire building, but at least a lot of dead people, since he'll have backup."

He took a couple of minutes to explain the situation.

"Damn," Davion offered once James finished. "That's even more fucked up than I had guessed. You want me to start tracing the girl's phone? I can't wait for you to deliver a Brownstone beat down to that asshole. I need to record it and put it on the net so people know what happens when they mess with you."

"Don't bother trying to trace it," James replied. "This

wizard wants physical cash from me, which means he's careful enough to block the normal shit, and he already knows I have infomancers helping me. I bet that phone's halfway to another country already, but he's still worried, which means we can get him. There's some hole we can exploit."

"How do you know he's worried?" Davion asked. "I mean, no offense, brah, but this ass is trying to extort money from the Granite Ghost. He's either crazy, or he's got balls of steel. Either way, it doesn't sound like the kind of dude who worries about stuff. I'd be wetting my pants if I had called you up and said the kind of stuff he said to you."

"He made a mistake with the drop-off location. That reveals everything I need to know about him."

"Amazing Dwayne's?" Davion sounded dubious. "What's so special about there? The pizza is trash, brah. I went to this party for the kid of this girl I was dating a few years back, and I was like, 'Man, why you feeding kids this pizza?'"

"I know he's afraid since the cowardly fucker is making me meet him in a kids' restaurant," James explained. He checked his mirrors in case any suspicious wizards had been stupid enough to wander over to the apartment. Two young men stumbled past his truck on the sidewalk, swaying and red-faced, too drunk to care enough to look his way.

"He knows I can't make a serious move there," he continued, "but that also means he's gonna be vulnerable and make some sort of appearance, or a lackey will. I need whatever evidence you can get without tipping him off. If we screw this up, he might kill Calista. The fucker is gonna die either way, but I'm saving her."

"Got you." Davion hummed for a few seconds. "The way I see it, this kidnapper asshole can't be that good at infomancy if he's afraid to take his payment in crypto coins, which means if I just do this old-fashioned and avoid any scrying, I might be able to pick something up we can use. I'll hack every camera in the area. I'll also get a bunch of drones going at different altitudes, maybe even hit up a few satellites, but just so you know, this might get the attention of the alphabet agencies. I'm willing to do it, but I don't know how much heat you want."

"I don't give a shit." James grunted. "Those fuckers are all afraid of me, and I can explain it to them later. This wizard is screwing with me, my orphanage, and my parish, and if he was trying to pay Calista to seduce me, that means that fucker thought he could blackmail me, and fuck with my marriage, too. If Shay wasn't so pregnant, she would be the one fucking them up, and you don't want an angry Shay after your ass."

Davion whistled. "Damn. When you put it like that, I almost feel sorry for the epic-level beat down he has coming. Almost. But you need to teach him a lesson."

"I will," James rumbled. "But I need your help to do it. So, can you help?"

"I'm going to do my best, brah, but if this guy is as careful as you say, he might be prepared for all that. There are plenty of spells he can use to beat cameras and shit, and if I can't go full magic, I can't guarantee results. I'm not trying to be all humble, I'm being real since that girl's life is in danger." Davion sighed.

James furrowed his brow as he considered the possibilities. "Understood, and I appreciate it. You just prepare to do your part. I don't want the whole agency involved in this shit because it'll get too dangerous for Calista, but I've got someone else who might be able to help."

———

Shay sighed on the couch and shook her head as James finished explaining the situation. "I hate being right all the time." She pointed to her stomach. "If I wasn't about to pop, I'd be on my way to arm up, track this guy down, and cut off his dick for trying to fuck with our family."

This fucker doesn't know how lucky he is it's just me coming for him. At least I'll finish him off quickly.

James paced the living room. Thomas followed him and wagged his tail, picking up on the energy but not the anger. "I wish this was simple stalker shit like you said first. This is the problem when I don't beat any fuckers down for a while. People get the idea they can come at me. That they can come at us. I'm gonna kill this fucker either way, but if I drop that money off, I've got no guarantee he'll let Calista go. She didn't do anything to deserve getting involved, other than knowing me. But I don't know an easy way to beat this guy. He's prepared more than most people I deal with."

Shay ran her tongue along the inside of her cheek. "Maybe…"

"Maybe what?" James frowned. "I know what you said, but you can't get anywhere near this. It's too much of a risk."

"That's not what I was thinking about. I'm not exactly at my most agile right now, even if I've been keeping in shape." Shay grinned. "I've got something else in mind. Remember that tomb raid under the abandoned nuke silo in Nebraska I did with Lily a few years back?"

James nodded slowly, not sure where she was going with her train of thought. "Yeah, there was some stuff you thought might be alien, but it turned out just to be, like, fossilized dragon crap. I don't think dragon shit's gonna help."

Shay made a face. "I'll have you know it has a lot of value to certain magicals, and I don't have any of that left. We made a lot of money off that job." She waved a hand. "But forget dragons. Remember what else I found? Unless your near-perfect memory is suddenly failing you?"

James shrugged. "You just said you found a few other minor artifacts. You didn't explain more, and I didn't care enough to ask. I always figure if I need to know, you'll tell me."

"They were more than just minor artifacts," Shay explained. "When I got them IDed, a few of them seemed like they would be useful, so I kept them, but the particular situations in which they might come in handy haven't come up yet. We've both got a lot of ways to track people, and one of them in particular is focused on that sort of thing."

"What is it?" James asked, curious now. "And how can it help us?"

Shay's grin grew wider, almost vulpine. "Don't worry. You'll find out when we go grab it from the warehouse. I'm sure you'll love it. As for how, it'll allow you to track something without the magical signature of the beacon being detected by most common types of magic. I don't know how it works, exactly. Some sort of dangerous magic was involved in its creation, and from what I understand, we can only get a few uses out of it before it dies."

James grunted. "Sounds annoying."

"Sure, but it'll work. And this is as good a time as any to use it." Shay shrugged. "Do you want to save that girl, or do you want to have an annoyance-free day?"

"Fine. Got anything you can think of that I can use to protect Calista at a distance?" James asked. "When this shit gets rough, the first thing they'll do is grab her to use as a human shield. I might not be able to get close enough to give her a ring or a necklace or anything like that."

Shay tapped her lips, looking down as she thought, then snapped her fingers. "I'm so fucking brilliant. If we weren't already married, you'd have to marry me because I'm so damned impressive."

"Huh?" James narrowed his eyes. A cocky Shay was a dangerous Shay, but that was a good thing, given who the target of her wrath was.

She winked. "I've got a better idea than shielding her. We're going to give this jolly asshole a reason to not care about her at all. That way, you can do your thing without any worries."

A smiling banker placed the last stack of wrapped bills in James' open briefcase. Two security guards stood outside the small room, hands on the grips of their guns. The door was locked, although considering who was making the withdrawal, a robbery would be suicidal.

"And that makes two million, Mr. Brownstone." The banker licked his lips, obvious excitement in his eyes. "All in cash. Would you like me to count it again?" It sounded more like pleading than an inquiry.

I wonder how often this guy gets to personally handle this much cash?

James shook his head. "I watched. It's all there." He reached across the table and closed the briefcase. "Thanks for getting this taken care of so quickly."

"Of course." The man placed a hand over his heart. "When I heard that it was *you* who needed the help, I personally pledged to make sure we would get this taken care of as quickly as possible. I understand a man of your background often is involved in complicated situations that don't lend themselves to normal procedures and times. Your license helps facilitate things, but I must again remind you that this transaction will be reported to the Treasury Department." He looked contrite. "I apologize if that causes you any inconvenience, but unfortunately, there's nothing we can do about that, even with your class-six license. It's unlikely, but they might end up contacting you."

"That's fine. This isn't anything they'll be interested in."

Yeah. It's more an FBI or PDA thing. This shit will all be over by the time the government comes sniffing around, and I doubt they're gonna pitch a fit about a dead kidnapper and extortionist.

The banker tilted his head, his eyes locked on the briefcase "I'm not one to tell you how to do your business, Mr. Brownstone, but you *are* aware that there's no DNA lock on this case, right? Most of our clients who make high-value withdrawals either use couriers with such cases or provide their own. I understand that you're, well, *you*, but accidents happen. Things can get misplaced, and this is a hell of a thing to misplace."

James shook his head. "A DNA lock would complicate things. I need this to be easily accessible and checkable for what I have in mind."

The banker leaned forward with a sly smile, his eyes darting back and forth. "You can level with me," he whispered. "Is this for some super-special bounty mission? Maybe to bribe an evil government official in a corrupt government so you can take down some evil necromancer?" He winked. "You can tell me. Consider it a banker's confidence. I won't tell anyone, not even the feds."

It's been a while since I beat down a necromancer. And it's been a long time since anyone tried to make me pay them a bribe.

"Nope," James offered. "Not a bounty. This money isn't leaving LA while I have it. I'm not taking any trips right now. My wife's about to give birth."

"Oh, yes, I'd forgotten about that." The man sighed and sat up. His breath caught. "Wait. I know what it is." He pointed at James. "You're going to pay for some rare meat. Something imported from Oriceran, perhaps? Barbequed unicorn or something?"

James made a face. He had no idea what unicorn tasted like, but there were certain things he wouldn't eat, regardless of how tasty they might be.

Shit. Now I'm wondering what unicorn tastes like. Thanks.

"It'd have to be the best damned barbeque in existence for me to pay two million dollars for the meat," he explained. He glanced down at the case. He needed to feed the man something before he spread too many rumors that might complicate things or get the police or government involved. "I'm thinking about buying a..." He frowned. "A yacht. Yeah, a yacht. I've got a lot of money, right? This is a down payment. I heard on some channel that yachts are a good investment, and I've been trying to figure out ways to spread my investments around. It might be fun to sail around the world one summer or something like that, you know?"

"I see. I suppose I can understand that." The banker sighed, disappointment spreading across his face in a creeping wave over the banal explanation for the withdrawal. "If that's all you're doing, I should point out we could have easily set up an electronic transfer for you. It would be far safer than carrying two million dollars in a briefcase without a DNA lock." His eyes widened. "Wait. Does it have a magic lock?"

"Nope, it's just a plain-old briefcase. I bought it at an office supply store before I came here. The one about six blocks down."

"Oh. I see." The banker's expression turned dour with James' continued slaying of his fantasies.

"As for an electronic transfer, I like the personal touch." James pulled the briefcase over to him and patted it. "Nothing like slapping a case full of cash in front of someone."

Yeah, a certain wizard's gonna experience my personal touch.

CHAPTER SEVEN

The magnificent cacophony created by scores of yelling children assaulted James' ears as he stepped inside Amazing Dwayne's. It was his first visit, and he hoped it would be his last. He'd never been more grateful that Alison was already a teenager when he'd first met her. It'd saved him from the sheer annoyance of concentrated childhood joy like the pizza place.

A sickening realization crept in, twisting his stomach. Some challenges couldn't be met with pure force. His new child wouldn't come out a teenager. He might be forced to come to annoying places like this in the future. A chat with Shay about forbidden restaurants needed to be placed on his near-term agenda. They should stick to barbeque joints.

High possibility of collateral damage from any initiation of battle, Whispy sent. *Human offspring lack sufficient tactical and situational awareness to minimize danger.*

James had bonded the symbiont on his way. Mr. Jolly Wizard hadn't specifically warned him not to use any of his personal tools, and there was no way he was walking into the situation without his primary advantage. The whole thing might come down to him having to take a hit for Calista.

I know all that, James thought. *We're not fighting anyone in here. We're just here to drop off the money and, if we're lucky, catch sight of the bastard who thinks he can jerk me around. Then we'll track him down, and we'll kill him.*

Recommend quick termination.

Yeah. Recommendation accepted.

Whispy's satisfaction filtered into James' mind. The symbiont might be obsessed with improvement above everything else, but his basic bloodthirst would always remain.

The briefcase felt light in James' hand, even with the two million dollars inside. He'd thought about pulling some sort of stunt and filling it with paper, but he doubted that would fool the wizard. A couple million to save a life wasn't necessarily too expensive, but there was no way he could let a magical kidnapper run around thinking he could kidnap people and extort money from James Brownstone. Like the wizard had said, two million dollars could have easily been twenty million. The principle remained the same.

The loud restaurant was divided into two major sections, along with a small counter in the back where you put in orders for pizzas and grabbed your fountain drinks. An arcade with different games was separated by a short wall from a dining area filled with long blue tables. A few gaps allowed passage between the two sections.

The arcade games were a mixture of VR, with headsets

and gloves awaiting players, and less immersive entertainment with more basic interfaces. Other games filled a smaller section near the back. Two children batted a glowing disc back and forth over a translucent beach scene. He wasn't sure if it was a hologram, magic, or something else.

My kid won't need that shit. My kid will have fun on the obstacle course I'm gonna build in the backyard.

James frowned. He should have started building it several months ago, but it didn't matter. It'd take a while for the kid to learn to walk anyway. He had time.

Children and their haggard-looking parents sat at the tables munching on different types of pizza. They all watched four wooden automatons playing Oriceran instruments. Despite the exaggerated cartoonish features and bright colors of the automatons, one was obviously supposed to be a flute-playing Light Elf woman. Another was a gnome male wearing a top hat. He blew into a reed atop a strange pyramidal wooden instrument that sounded like the bastard child of an oboe and a trombone. The band included a rat-like Willen playing a single hand drum and a centaur plucking an instrument that approximated a lute. The gnome and the Willen sang a loud song about friendship. According to art on the wall, the Willen character was supposed to be the eponymous Amazing Dwayne.

An illustrated story near the front informed James that the Amazing Dwayne had traveled all the way from Oriceran after getting a taste of pizza, and now wanted to "share the joy of song and pizza" with Earth children.

They look fake. Is that because it's easier to do that kind of thing, or do they want to make people forget this is actually magic and not robots? I'm surprised a gnome would make something like this, but maybe he figured it was a good way to make a quick buck.

A smiling young woman stepped forward. Her uniform was a riot of colors and covered with what James assumed were drawings of the Amazing Dwayne's band. Her name tag read Devon.

Only a flicker of hesitation appeared on her face before she announced, "Welcome to Amazing Dwayne's, a touch of magic, and pizza so delicious it must be enchanted. Are we a party of one today, or are you waiting for more people?" She didn't give any indication she recognized James. Her gaze dropped to the briefcase, suspicion sneaking into her happy façade.

"I'm not here for pizza," James replied, menace seeping into his voice. He was too annoyed to lie. "I'm looking for someone. I'm supposed to give them something here." He raised the case.

The woman winced. He felt bad. It wasn't her fault he'd been forced into a loud kids' restaurant for a ransom drop-off. If anything, he felt pity for her. Having to spend eight to twelve hours a day around hundreds of screaming kids was something that might even challenge Whispy's adaptation ability.

"Um, okay, sir," Devon offered slowly, glancing over her shoulder at another employee. "I suppose you could sit..." She looked around and pointed to an empty table—the second closest to the entrance.

Did Mr. Jolly Wizard do something to keep the table clear?

"There for a few minutes," she continued, "but if it's going to be more than that, we're going to have to at least ask you to buy a drink. This isn't a park." She squinted, a flicker of confusion passing over her face.

"Fine," James rumbled. He stepped past her. Small children swarmed past him on their way to their waving parents in the dining area. With a grunt, he sat down at the table and set the briefcase on the top. He alternated between watching the entrance and surveying the restaurant. The table didn't offer great visibility. Another plan, perhaps.

Estimated tactical combat potential of all human offspring present minimal, Whispy noted, a hint of derision leaking into James' mind. *Host offspring will have far superior battle potential than normal human offspring.*

What's that supposed to mean? James thought. *Did you do something to my kid?*

Heritability of key genetic compatibility elements doesn't require major active alteration of basic DNA.

Heritability? James thought.

A little girl rushed past his table and skidded to a halt a few feet away. She turned and stared at James wide-eyed.

This conversation isn't over, Whispy, James sent. *We'll get back to it.*

"What?" he rumbled at the girl. He didn't care about being gawked at, but he didn't need to be distracted when he was looking for wizards to kill.

She jerked her finger up. "You!"

"What about me?" James took a deep breath. This was good practice for his future child. Intimidating some random kid wasn't useful for bounties or his restaurant, but learning to tolerate annoying and random children's behavior would be helpful for a number of years. He couldn't always bully his kid into silence. All the podcasts said so.

"Mommy, look!" the girl shouted. She bounced as she pointed at him. "It's the man from the news. The I-5 Hero."

Shit. Stupid news.

A middle-aged woman with a stylish bob and a disapproving look who was sitting a few yards away moved closer, wrinkling her nose in disgust as she looked him over. A moment later, she smiled.

"Wait," she declared. "She's right. You're James Brownstone." Her warm smile seemed almost genuine.

James scrubbed a hand down his face. He didn't have time for this shit. "Yeah, I'm James Brownstone."

The woman cleared her throat and reached into her purse, producing a pen and a small piece of paper. "My husband is a huge fan of yours. He would just *die* if I could get your autograph. He's been to your restaurant so many times, but he's been too afraid to ask for it." She rolled her eyes. "He's not a real man like you."

James sighed and accepted the pen and paper. "Fine." He scribbled his autograph. Years of being in the situation combined with a lack of care had reduced the signature to something more resembling an erratic EKG reading than anything intelligible.

Several other adults stampeded toward the table, eager for autographs, almost knocking over some kids. Packs of children joined them.

"I think he's that guy from the movie," a kid explained to another.

"No, he's that football player," challenged another.

Devon joined the line, an eager smile replacing her confusion and suspicion.

James looked at the burgeoning crowd. He didn't spot anyone with a wand, but the kidnapper could easily have used a spell to hide their appearance. This was why he hated magic. It was complicated by its very nature.

At least all these people wanting autographs gives me an excuse to stay for a few more minutes. Jolly's got to be watching this place, but maybe he'll get too eager and slip up.

"Come on." James gestured to the closest person. "Let's get signing."

Where the fuck are you, Mr. Jolly Wizard? If you're so prepared, why not put in an appearance?

The crowd thinned as the minutes passed and children found more entertainment in the arcade, eating pizza, or singing along with the band than watching a scowling man signing pieces of paper or virtual signing on phones. James continued scribbling his autograph. The briefcase remained unmolested in front of him on the table.

Maybe this guy's not gonna be dumb enough to make the grab while I'm here. I'm going to need to watch it. Davion's got the feeds going, so it's time to make my move and force Jolly to go for it.

James waved Devon down. She jogged over to him, hope on her face.

He patted the suitcase. "Someone's coming to get this, so is it all right if I leave it here for a few minutes? I've got an appointment."

"Sure," the girl replied, batting her eyes. "Anything for you, Mr. Brownstone. Thanks for coming to Amazing Dwayne's today."

James stood and scanned the restaurant one last time. By then, almost all of the children and adults had returned to their pre-Brownstone entertainment. That didn't surprise him. Everyone knew James Brownstone was good for an autograph, but not the kind of man who would offer interesting anecdotes on command for fans.

At least they aren't as annoying as that guy who used to live next to Alison. Crazy fanboy.

James headed toward the door, keeping the briefcase at the edge of his peripheral vision. The automatons continued to sing, dance, and play, offering their peppy take on why children shouldn't be picky eaters, which was ironic, considering the location. When James was a few feet from the door, they swiveled to the side. A loud screech erupted from all four of their mouths, overriding all sound in the room. An impressive achievement, given the child horde.

The gathered children yelped in surprise, many covering their ears. Several adults glared at a nearby employee, who shrugged in response, looking just as confused as they were. Devon sighed and rolled her eyes.

James spun to face the automatons directly. "What the hell?"

The magical band all turned toward him. It was hard to tell with their huge eyes, but it felt like they were staring directly at him.

I better not get attacked by a bunch of giant singing dolls. That would just be obnoxious.

Likely tactical capability limited, Whispy reported.

It's more about me having to explain it to Shay later. She'll make jokes about it for months.

"When you're mad, things get bad," sang the gnome, slightly off-key. So much for the power of magic.

"You shouldn't be mad. You should be glad," continued the Willen, his voice higher than the gnome's. He pounded his drum. His tail twitched.

The band played a festive, jaunty tune for a few measures. The confusion began to fade from the faces of the children and parents. They returned to eating their pizza and chatting amongst themselves.

Devon frowned and shrugged at another employee near the entrance. "I don't know this song. Do you know this song?"

"Nope. I wonder if they're malfunctioning again. We can't have a repeat of the heavy metal incident." The second employee sighed. "Now we're going to have to call corporate and wait until the repair wizard can show up. It took him a week last time. So many bitching parents. I'm thinking, 'Lady, do I look like a wizard to you? If I knew magic, I wouldn't be putting up with your shit.'"

The employees grimaced when they realized James had overheard them, but he ignored them and focused on the eerie automatons.

"When you're glad," sang the gnome, "you'll gain a new friend."

The Willen swayed. "And now, Mr. Brownstone, this song is at an end."

The four automatons all slumped forward. Everyone turned to look at James.

Okay, what the fuck was that? Oh, shit.

James jerked his head toward the table. The briefcase was gone. He rushed out of the restaurant. The parking lot was filled with cars, but there wasn't anyone there, and no sign of the briefcase. There was also no sign of Calista.

"Davion," he rumbled. "What do you have?"

"That was weird, brah," the infomancer replied through James' hidden ear receiver. "The camera feeds died for like a couple of seconds when those things were singing that song about you. I was sticking to passive magical detection, and there was definitely a magical surge before that screech. There's still a huge background cloud of magic. I'm getting a feel for its signature, but it's not something I can track."

"And? Any vehicles? Portals? Anything?"

Davion sucked in a breath. "Sorry. Every car that was there before then is still there. No weird readings, no one inside of them. That cloud is starting to go away, but the problem is, if they did a spell, I might not be able to pick up on it unless it was major. It's a huge waste of magical energy, but it's a good way of cloaking stuff."

James clenched his hands into fists. "They got the money, but we don't have Calista."

"I'm sorry."

"It's not you I'm pissed at. We thought this might happen. You did what you could. Now it's time for Shay's backup plan." A feral grin took over James' face. "The asshole is too fucking cocky. That stunt with the band wasn't cute. Time to find him and tell him what I thought of his song."

CHAPTER EIGHT

James gripped the wheel of his rental Subaru SUV as he drove down the street. A mixture of embarrassment and anger was flowing through him, both over his temporary vehicle choice and the artifact Shay had given him.

"I can't believe this is what I'm using," he mumbled.

"You talking about the car or the artifact?" Davion transmitted.

"Both."

"It's a pretty sweet artifact, brah," Davion transmitted. "And it's not like you're keeping the car. The artifact's still working, right?"

"Yeah." James glanced at his dash. "It's still working. Annoying as fuck, but it's working."

A small toy monkey in a yellow vest holding cymbals sat atop the dash, clanging away every few seconds. From what Shay had explained, the monkey was a very specific type of tracking artifact. It clanged at a higher tempo, the closer it was to a paired tiny toy banana. The target banana couldn't be detected by most standard spells, meaning he needed to cruise around town with the freaking monkey constantly clanging its damned cymbals to find the brief-case with the hidden banana. The annoyance was offset by the fact that the monkey could track the banana through most types of wards. He didn't understand the magical theory behind it, and neither did Shay, but they didn't have to for it to work.

Since the F-350 was too famous and obvious, James had switched to a rental car with the help of Davion, who had used a few cloaking and misdirection spells. For now, the truck sat in a long-term parking lot, awaiting his return. If Mr. Jolly Wizard was trying hard, he might have been able to pierce some of the spells the infomancer had whipped up, but it was not likely without Davion figuring it out and informing James. As annoying as James found the info-mancer, he rarely questioned his skills. Davion's fleet of drones also patrolled the skies, looking for any sign of Calista and trying to help James triangulate the banana's location.

Whispy remained quiet, the occasional flare of blood-lust and irritation bubbling up. James didn't want to follow up on their earlier conversation about what he might have done to the kid just yet. He didn't want to be distracted while he was getting ready to kill someone. Or a whole group of people.

The minutes passed, the monkey's enthusiasm increasing in tandem with James' annoyance. Davion and the monkey's guidance had soon narrowed the likely loca-tion to Beverly Hills. There were several mansions in the area that radiated high levels of magic, but that didn't mean anything in and of itself. Rich Oricerans liked living in nice neighborhoods as much as rich humans. Some of the mutual distrust disappeared when both groups thought of themselves as elite.

James drove by a particular mansion a third time, the monkey going wild. "Looks like we found it."

"I'm keeping the drones flying semi-random paths and high," Davion explained. "If they leave any other way than a portal, I'll spot them. You just go do your thing, and I'll make sure they don't get away. But it's definitely that place. The magical signature is the same as at Amazing Dwayne's."

Ready, Whispy? James sent

Who are we going to kill today? the symbiont asked.

Same guy. Someone who made poor life choices. A wizard.

Terminate quickly. Low new adaptation potential.

James pulled into the long, smooth driveway and stopped in front of the large metal gate. An intercom was embedded in a squat metal pole rising from the ground on the left side of the drive. After a moment, he veered to the right side and parked the car. He exited the vehicle, sparing it a quick glance. He'd picked something cheaper in case it got blown up. No rental company had been willing to give him extra insurance for a long time. He suspected the only reason they even bothered to rent vehicles to him on the rare occasion he needed one was that he was quick to pay for damaged rentals.

Fuck that. I need to focus.

He walked over to the intercom and pressed the call button. He tugged on his shabby gray coat. It'd been a while since he'd gone through one. It bore a minimum load today. He wasn't even carrying his .45. A small weight rested in a right outer pocket, a golden derringer that was a little surprise for Mr. Jolly Wizard. Other weapons weren't necessary. His claws and blades would do the rest.

"Who's this?" a man barked over the intercom.

"You know who the fuck this is, dumbass," James yelled. "Don't play fucking games. Just let me in, or I'll come in through the damned wall anyway, you asshole. I'm already pissed. The only reason I haven't blown up that whole fucking place is that Calista might be in there. If she isn't, you'll be dead in the next few minutes."

"Wait," the other man replied.

About ten seconds later, the gate buzzed and parted. James stomped through and headed toward straight to the wide veranda. He'd expected snipers or a few explosions along the way, maybe even a few lawn monsters, but nothing ambushed him during his short hike between the gate and the veranda stairs. The door opened as he stepped onto the porch and he passed through it into an empty marble-floored foyer. The foyer fed into a massive living room.

Calista, pale and unconscious but breathing, lay on one of the four grand leather couches in the center of the otherwise mostly empty space. A few sheets had been draped over some furniture pushed against the wall.

A man in a black tuxedo with a long black wand in his hand stood behind Calista's couch. Between the tux and the black wand, he only needed a top hat to look like a stage magician. More plainly dressed larger men in jeans and t-shirts were arrayed behind him, but their simple appearance was offset by the glowing arcane glyphs covering their faces and exposed arms.

"You must be Mr. Jolly Wizard," James rumbled. "I'd say nice to meet you, but that seems pointless since I'm about to kill you."

Engage the enemy, Whispy insisted. *Kill the enemy. Increase terror of potential enemies. Low adaptation potential suggests quick termination is recommended course of action.*

That's the idea, James thought.

The tuxedo-clad wizard laughed. "Mr. Jolly Wizard? I go by many names, but you can call me Jonathan if you want."

James raised a hand and clenched it into a fist in front of his chest. "We had a fucking deal, Jonathan. I gave you two million dollars, and you were supposed to give me the girl. Instead, you pulled that shit with those singing toys and kept the girl. Now I'm trying to figure out why I shouldn't kill your ass right away. The only reason I'm coming up with is it might be nice for you to be afraid for a while before I kill you."

"Thank you for the money." Jonathan crouched behind the couch. When he stood, he held the briefcase in his hand. "I'm impressed on one level that you were able to track me." He set the briefcase down before reaching into a pocket and pulling out the tiny banana. He held it between two fingers. "This is an interesting little toy. I assumed you were going to track me somehow, but I couldn't figure out how. It wasn't until I noticed the obvious lack of magic that I found this hidden in the lining. I admit I underestimated your resourcefulness."

He tossed it on the ground and pointed his wand, then

chanted a quick spell and zapped the banana with a black bolt. The artifact turned to ash.

Shit. Well, Shay said it only would only work a few times anyway.

"If you knew I would be able to track you, why all the games?" James asked. "Why the restaurant crap?"

"Because it was interesting?" Jonathan shrugged, the smug look on his face more than enough for James to want to kill him, even without all the other valid reasons. "Consider it a test. You're famous for both your battle prowess and your ability to find people. I figured if you couldn't find me, I would have two million dollars and the girl, and if you could find me? Well, I'd still have two million dollars and the girl, but I'd just treat it as good-faith money."

James clenched teeth and squared his shoulders. "Good-faith money?"

"Why not?" Jonathan replied cheerfully. "I didn't think it would be this easy, and since it has been, I might as well ask for more. I told you before. You're a wealthy man who doesn't spend a lot of his money anymore. Why not donate it to me? Money sitting around doesn't do anyone any good, and it's not like I've hurt the girl yet, other than a few minor injuries."

Kill the enemy, Whispy insisted.

Almost there. Don't worry.

James gestured around the sprawling room. "You already have a mansion, asshole. You're rich. Why do you need more money?"

Jonathan smiled. "I'm borrowing the mansion, but a man can always use more money, especially when it's not his."

"I'm not giving you any more money." James glared at him. "But I will fuck you up."

The wizard laughed and pointed his wand at Calista. "There's no way you can, as you so crudely put it, 'fuck me up' without this girl dying. Are you ready for that, Mr. Brownstone? You're the man who took in an orphan and killed her father for his betrayal. You faced off against a monster in Las Vegas to avenge other children. You spent years secretly and then openly giving money to help children. I've found your weakness, and I'm exploiting it. If you want to be angry, be mad at yourself for being so easy to manipulate. This girl's life is in your hands now, not mine. You have to decide what is more important, her life or some money. I would think the choice is easy."

Pride, fucker. And falls.

James reached into a pocket and pulled out a small golden derringer. "You think you can control me that easily?"

Jonathan stepped back with a lopsided grin. "Just because you can't see it doesn't mean I didn't shield myself." His thugs spread out, scowls consuming their faces. "Maybe you need to understand the stakes better." He whispered a spell. A quick flash surrounded Calista, and she groaned, her eyes opening.

"Mr. Brownstone?" The girl sat up and clutched her stomach. Her eyes widened. "You're here!" She looked both grateful and surprised.

The wizard clucked his tongue. "A young woman in the prime of her early life. After such adversity, she has a chance to make something of herself. Wouldn't it be a shame if she died here?" The casual happiness infusing his tone made the declaration that much more sickening. "Here's how it's going to work. Her price just doubled. I'm going to send some of my men with you for more money. You'll bring it back here, and I'll let her leave. I might want some money in the future, but I can be reasonable."

Whispy's murder request was nearly a drumbeat in James' mind.

"You don't understand," James replied.

"What don't I understand?" Jonathan asked.

"I can't let anyone blackmail or extort me." James raised the derringer, pointing it at Calista. "It sets a bad precedent. Anyone who thinks they can will try to push my family and me, and I'm supposed to be retired. If I have to deal with this kind of shit, it'll mean I can't concentrate on my restaurant and wife and kids. I'm supposed to only be worrying about fucking barbeque."

The girl's eyes widened. "Mr. Brownstone?"

I trust you, Shay, James thought. *But I really don't like having to put her through this.*

Jonathan threw his head back and laughed. "Oh, please. Do you really think I would fall for that? You're trying to tell me you're going to shoot an innocent girl rather than give me money? How stupid do you think I am? Stop this pathetic farce and put the gun down."

The surprisingly loud report of the derringer echoed throughout the room. Calista's body jerked and she slumped forward, her arms under her body. The gun darkened and cracked. James tossed it on the ground.

"Wait." Jonathan blinked several times, then stared at Calista. "What? Impossible. That's not a normal gun. I felt magic. What did you do?"

"I had to be sure." James shifted his gaze from Calista to the wizard. "I needed to remove the shield you were hiding behind. I told you. I can't allow some things. You've pushed me too far, and now you're gonna pay for that."

"What magic? What spell?" Jonathan swallowed.

"Don't worry about it," James growled, and his nostrils flared. "You're gonna be dead soon enough. You can ask the Devil about it in hell."

Kill the enemy, Whispy shouted.

Yeah. Let's do that.

His family. His friends. His church. His orphanage. His town.

The underworld was supposed to understand one simple fact: they didn't mess with his world. If they didn't, he *might* not fuck theirs up. But if they stepped over the line, they weren't allowed to beg to go back to the way things were. It was time for a refresher lesson.

"You thought you could get away with this shit?" James asked, glaring at the wizard. "You thought you could throw that girl at me and make me cheat on my wife? You just said all that shit about how you studied my life, and *that* was your plan? You dumbass piece of shit."

Jonathan stepped back and pointed his wand at James. "You're still outnumbered, Mr. Brownstone." His voice quivered. "Your victory isn't assured."

"You studied my life. You sure of that?"

"I've already enchanted my guards," Jonathan noted. "We were prepared and waiting for you."

"You thought you could threaten to burn down my fucking orphanage and murder priests from my church, and I wouldn't fucking find out and kill you?" James yelled.

Heat suffused his body. His heart galloped as Whispy screamed for blood. "I'll give you credit for one thing."

"What's that?" Hope crept into Jonathan's voice. The poor fool actually thought he might survive. A sliver of pity pricked James before being washed away by the torrent of anger.

"You did something that's hard to do anymore. You got me not just annoyed, but really fucking pissed. Good for me. I don't have to waste an artifact. Bad for you, because I don't know if I'm gonna rein it in this time. There might not be much of you left when this is all done."

"W-we can work something out, Mr. Brownstone," Jonathan insisted, sweat beading on his forehead. "I-I can pay you."

"You just got done saying how I had a bunch of money I don't need," James rumbled. "Why would I need more?"

Power sufficient for extended advanced transformation, Whispy reported.

Good. Time to kill.

Tendrils shot from the amulet, coating James' body until it finished growing the silver-green biometallic armor, which proved too much for his clothes. The thick armor challenged the seams of the coat. He tore it off and tossed it to the ground as his helmet sealed around him, his now-wider vision returning after a few seconds. A blade extended from his right forearm and claws grew from his hands.

James roared. The wizard and his thugs flinched.

"Time to die, Jonathan."

CHAPTER NINE

Jonathan stepped back, some of the fear vanishing off his face. He grinned. "Okay, there it is. I'll admit it scared me a little, but now that I understand you use magic objects that don't emit magic somehow, it's easier to deal with you." He reached into his jacket pocket and pulled out a small dart. "Remember, I did study you, Mr. Brownstone, and I knew you wouldn't reach maximum danger until you put on your magic armor."

James stomped forward, growling. "If you come here and get on your knees, I'll kill you quickly. You might die quickly otherwise, but no guarantees."

The wizard held up the dart. "You know about this?"

The thugs exchanged nervous looks.

"I don't give a fuck," James snarled.

"You're not the only ones with artifacts, Mr. Brownstone." Jonathan threw the dart into the air and whipped up his wand. He chanted off a quick spell, and the dart shot toward James, exploding in a cloud of thick green mist around him. "In a few seconds, all your magic will be suppressed, and then I'm going to kill you and become the most feared man in Los Angeles. Maybe even the country."

James took a step out of the mist. "There's something you need to understand. Something that all your fucking research didn't tell you."

The wizard kept a smile on his face, but he stepped behind some of the thugs. "What's that?"

"This shit isn't magic." James flew across the room, his blade pointed down.

Blood splattered on the ground as he landed on top of a thug, his blade poking through his head. He yanked out the weapon and stood, whipping the blood off his weapon.

"Damn it," Jonathan muttered. He raised his wand, rattling off another spell.

A fiery nimbus surrounded two of the thugs closest to James. They both charged him and threw flaming punches and kicks. The blows barely registered. He might as well have been attacked by kids from the restaurant.

Maximum adaptation already achieved, Whispy reported.

James decapitated the men with two quick swipes of his blade. He roared as their headless bodies collapsed to the ground. Jonathan pelted him with a fireball and a quick blast of lightning. They blackened his armor but didn't penetrate.

"Take him down!" Jonathan screamed.

The men hesitated.

James didn't move. "Go ahead and try. If you run, I'll kill you anyway. No one leaves this room alive today."

One of the thugs sprinted for the door. James leapt on top of him, tearing into him with his claws. The crunching and ripping were over in seconds, leaving a mangled corpse missing most of its center.

"You will all die because you helped him," James growled.

Jonathan rapidly chanted under his breath. A bright glow surrounded him, following by numerous small orbs. His men charged, screaming in fear and desperation.

James skewered one man before tearing the throat out of another. They pummeled him, their glyphs now flashing with each hit, different colors suffusing their fists.

Maximum adaptation achieved to existing attack types, Whispy reported.

One man met his fate by being sliced in half. Several more lost their heads. The closest James came to mercy was the few he stabbed through the heart. In less than a minute, the bodies of the enchanted thugs lay all over the blood-soaked floor. All their efforts and magical enhancements, and he'd felt almost nothing.

The wizard hadn't run. Hadn't attacked. He'd spent the entire short fight casting spell after spell on himself. Besides the energy fields surrounding him, a shiny golden sheen covered his skin.

"You're not the only one with tricks," Jonathan insisted, his voice trembling. He pointed his wand at the ground around James and shouted another spell. Several marble hands ripped from the floor and tightened around the raging Vax, who struggled but couldn't move.

"Ha!" The wizard let out a high-pitched laugh. "I win. Y-you can't kill what you can't even attack. You're strong, but are you strong enough to muscle out of marble?"

"You didn't study enough," James growled. "I've learned

my own tricks over the years." Lines of green energy danced and sparked on the blade, increasing in intensity. They shot from it and spread all over his body until a bright green glow surrounded him. A column of energy blasted from his body, vaporizing the marble hands and punching a hole through the ceiling.

"Woah," Davion transmitted. "Careful there, brah. That blast went pretty high."

James pointed his arm blade at the wizard. More energy cascaded down it. "You should have never even thought about it."

Jonathan screamed his incantations in rapid succession. A fireball and three different colors of magical rays erupted from his wand. All struck James square in the chest, but the armored man only grunted as he continued his own attack. The wizard's courage finally failed him, and he turned to run.

With Davion's words at the edge of his consciousness, James dropped to one knee and raised the angle of his arm. A blinding green beam erupted from his blade and incinerated the top half of the wizard's body. The rest of it tumbled to the ground, charred.

"Did I hit anything important?" James rumbled.

"Not sure," Davion replied. "One second. You didn't hit anything I can see."

No new adaptation gained from enemies, Whispy reported, his disappointment thick in James' mind.

Sometimes you just need to kill a few fuckers.

Acknowledged.

James took a few deep breaths. Jonathan had spun him

up enough to fuel his transformation, but James wasn't like he had been before. The blind rage of the past almost never took over. He was the master now, and the symbiont his servant. He retracted his claws, blade, and helmet before walking over to scoop up Calista.

"Your little light show got some attention," Davion explained. "AET is on the way, along with the cops."

"It's fine," James replied as he kicked open the front door. "This shit's all over anyway." He carried the girl out to the front lawn and laid her down before murmuring, "*Vylechit' sebya.*"

Calista's body glowed for a moment and she sat up, rubbing her forehead, her cheeks rosier than before. "W-what happened? It can't be. The last thing I remember is you shooting me."

"I did shoot you." James shrugged. "It's a healing gun, not a hurting gun."

She looked over at the house, uncertainty and fear in her eyes. "And the kidnappers?"

James hesitated for a moment. "I didn't want you to wake up to what I did, but they'll never kidnap or hurt anyone ever again. I handled it."

Calista sighed and nodded. She looked down. "I'm sorry, Mr. Brownstone. I wish I could have done something differently."

"No. I'm sorry you got caught up in all this. Next time, just tell me the truth right away, and I'll take care of it." James turned and looked at a dark blob flying low in the sky. "When the cops arrive, let me do the talking."

Shay fluffed her pillow before laying her head down. "And he had a bounty, too? You're a lucky son of a bitch, James Brownstone."

"Apparently, this guy specialized in kidnapping and extortion," James explained as he emerged from the bathroom, a minty fresh feeling from his toothpaste in his mouth. He wasn't even sure he needed to brush his teeth given his regeneration, but Whispy was unclear on the point, and he didn't want to end up with every part of him being tough except for dentures. "This honeypot shit was his specialty. He's done it to a bunch of politicians and CEOs. From what the cops told me, he normally doesn't go for so much money at once. That's one of the reasons he's gotten away with it. No one wants to be embarrassed, and he's not bleeding them dry."

"Uh-huh. And the cops aren't giving you any heat? Or the government? I know you didn't go Forerunner, but you blasted off your cannon in the city."

"The bounty wasn't dead-or-alive, so I'm not getting most of the reward, but the bounty, combined with Calista's statement, means they're treating it as self-defense and protection of the girl." James shrugged and slipped under the blanket. "From what Weber's telling me, the high-ups want it to go away anyway. I'm guessing Jonathan had a few victims in LA. I also took some money and splashed it around, so that everyone knows what happened and why it's a bad idea to fuck with me, even indirectly."

"It's over." Shay smiled. "I was worried this would turn into some weird stalker-fangirl thing, but idiot kidnappers? Always easier to solve. At least this way, I didn't have to solve it myself."

James frowned. "Meaning what?"

Shay gave him a wicked grin. "You're not the only one who is willing to use a little overkill to protect what's important."

CHAPTER TEN

James closed the F-350 and headed toward the door to the house. After the excitement with Jolly Jonathan, the following week had been free of trouble and full of customers. He'd experimented with a few new recipes at the restaurant, although with Earth meats. If *he* wasn't ready for magic cow, he doubted his regulars were either. Even Luis, who'd once claimed he'd eat a tire if James grilled it for him.

Maybe there's an Oriceran tire that tastes like pineapple.

James pulled out his phone and entered **Are there Oriceran tires that taste like pineapple?** into a search engine. He scanned the hits, but none looked promising.

He opened the door and stepped out of the garage, his head down as he strode toward the coat rack. He stuck his phone in his pants before pulling off his jacket. "What do you think I should do with the rest of the magic cow meat? Thomas didn't like it either."

"We should discuss that at a different time," Shay replied, tension in her voice.

James frowned.

She's been in a great mood since I wrapped up that Calista shit. Wait. It couldn't be? It's too early.

He turned to face her in the living room.

Shay stood in front of the couch, her skin glowing bright silver, a 9mm in her right hand and a flaming dagger in her left. Both weapons were pointed at a slender, pale, auburn-haired woman in a tight green sweater and black jeans. The woman, who looked to be in her mid-twenties, held her hands above her head. Most of her fingers bore a gold or silver ring inscribed with runes or glyphs. James wasn't sure which confused him more, the unseasonable fashion choice or his wife's readied weaponry.

Thomas lay curled up on James' chair, his eyes closed, oblivious to the tension. A mighty guard dog, indeed.

James whipped out his .45 and pointed it at the pale woman. If Shay was planning to kill someone, she probably had a good reason. "Where did you get that knife, Shay? You get kicked out of guarding the Garden of Eden?"

His wife laughed. "Seriously? *That's* what you want to ask me when you come home to this?"

"I haven't seen it before." James shrugged. The guest was already contained, so there was no reason to worry. Even weeks from birth, Shay could handle most threats.

"I didn't tell you?" Shay snickered. "I got it at the baby shower as a gift from Zoe."

"Interesting baby shower." James shook his gun at the other woman. "And who is she?"

The auburn-haired woman offered him a soft smile but didn't speak.

"That's the question of the hour," Shay replied. "I went

into the kitchen to get a snack, and when I came back out, she was here, so I grabbed my weapons. She refused to identify herself and said she was waiting for you."

Where was she even hiding that stuff?

The woman gently cleared her throat. "There's no need for weapons. I mean you no harm. You can't blame me for being a little curious, so I let myself in. I don't know what I was expecting." The woman looked around, running her tongue inside her cheek. "I didn't expect it to be fancy, but I don't know—more camouflage-y or something. Definitely more defensive magic, at least."

James grunted. Maybe he had a stalker problem after all.

Shay smirked at the woman. "You're mighty comfortable for a woman with two guns and a magic flaming knife pointed at her."

"I'm not trying to be a pompous bitch," the woman replied, shaking her hands. "But I doubt any of those weapons could hurt me."

James holstered his gun and slipped his hand under his shirt. He didn't pull the spacer off his amulet, but something in the woman's green eyes told him she wasn't bluffing. "You're threatening my pregnant wife?"

She waved her hands. "No, no, no. You're misinterpreting me. I'm only doing the hands-up thing because I didn't want to start a fight that would damage your home and piss either of you off. You both could probably kill me if you tried hard enough, just maybe not with those weapons. Let's be real, James. Can I call you, James? Anyway, if you got serious, I don't know if anyone on this planet could win against you." She smiled at Shay. "Can I lower my arms now? This is kind of annoying." She nodded toward the couch. "And that looks really comfy, and I'm sure you're not enjoying standing there ready to kill me, being preggers and all."

Shay locked eyes with the other woman. After a second, she jerked her gun toward the couch. "Fine. Take a seat. Do anything sudden, you die."

"You sure?" James asked, focused on the auburn-haired intruder.

"Yeah. Call it a killer mother's instinct." When Shay muttered something under her breath, her silver glow dissipated and the fire surrounding the dagger died out. "Thomas, get out of the chair, you sleepy old dog."

The dog perked up and bounded out, barking once, his tail wagging before walking over to sniff the red-haired woman's legs and feet.

"I'm Harper, by the way," the woman offered. She leaned over to scratch Thomas behind the ears. His tailed pounded on the floor before he wandered off to go drink from his bowl.

James pulled his hand out of his shirt, confused but willing to trust his wife's judgment. He didn't sit. Even without bonding Whispy, he could close the distance and knock Harper into the kitchen with ease. Her confidence suggested some sort of magical defense, but he didn't need to kill her on the first attack, just distract her long enough for Shay to reactivate her defenses.

Harper rubbed her hands together. "Wow. Tense, am I right?" She chuckled. "Sorry about all that. I have to say, I wouldn't be able to get out a gun and knife that quickly if I were ready to pop. Say, before we get into things, do you have any tea?"

"Do we look fucking English to you?" James rumbled.

"Americans drink tea, too," Harper replied with a faint pout.

"Who the fuck are you?" James demanded.

"Weren't you listening? I'm Harper."

"I know what your name is, but I don't know why the fuck you're in my house." James narrowed his eyes. "If you're some stalker fangirl, don't think I'm not calling the cops and getting your ass tossed in jail."

"Stalker fangirl?" Harper laughed, the sound light and breezy. She might be easy to like if she wasn't breaking into people's houses. "I appreciate your talents, James, but I'm not really the fangirl type."

"Then answer the question," Shay suggested. "Before we get more irritated than we already are or kill you anyway."

"I'm a magical courier." Harper scrunched her forehead and put a finger on her bottom lip. "I should be clearer. I'm not a *magical* courier. I'm a normal human courier who specializes in transporting magical things. In a previous life, when I used to do a little tomb raiding, I got my hands on some magical dampening artifacts. They've helped me carve out a bit of a niche in unstable-magic-type jobs. I'm a little different than a lot of high-value magical couriers because I'm always well aware of what I'm carrying since I need to know so I can safely transport it."

"A courier?" James folded his arms. "You're supposed to be delivering something to me? I didn't order anything."

Did Nadina send her? I don't want to eat any meat that

would require a special magical dampening courier to transport it.

Harper shook her head. "No, it's not that. It's more that I need your help on a job. I know you've helped high-value couriers in the past, and I figured, 'Hey, I'm in a bit of a jam. Why not go find the Granite Ghost and get him to help?'"

James grunted. "I don't work for fucking Andercarr or UPS. Yeah, I've helped couriers in the past, because I was doing a favor for close friends. I barely do bounties anymore, and you think you can bust into my house and ask me to help you? You should kick your dust habit if you're gonna walk around high all the time."

Harper placed her palms together with a pleading look on her face. "A teensy-weensy problem is all. My fancy magical dampening artifacts don't mean anything when it comes to excessive conventional threats or normal accidents. There was a little problem when I was flying, and it went down in Central Texas with some cargo. Some very dangerous cargo. Magical, if that's not obvious, and I need your help to handle it."

James shrugged. "So? Why should I care? Shouldn't you contact the PDA or FEMA about it?"

She sucked in a breath, discomfort on her face. "Yeah, I totally get where you're coming from, but I can't do that."

"Why?"

"The problem is, when I looked into things a bit more following the accident, I learned the people I was carrying the artifact for aren't the nicest. If I go to the authorities about this, I'm likely to end up in tiny little pieces." She pointed at her cheeks with both hands. "And when you're this adorable, that's a real waste."

Shay rolled her eyes. "Who's the client?"

Harper eyed Shay, her gaze calculating. "The Southguards."

Shay barked out a laugh. "Yeah, you're fucked. There won't even be pieces left of you when they're done."

"I know, right?" Harper sighed.

"Who the fuck are the Southguards?" James rumbled.

"Powerful family," Shay explained. "They've been trying to collect artifacts for centuries, and did a halfway decent job, even back when people like the Griffins were still sniffing around. The Southguards themselves aren't magicals, but they are completely ruthless and willing to use artifacts to secure their power. They don't think anything of killing whoever gets in their way. They're actually a little pissed that the gates started opening again because their artifact collection meant they had some parity with magicals."

James frowned at Harper. "Don't you normally check on who you're working for?"

Harper let out a little giggle. Her innocent act was starting to grate. "It kind of helps me sleep at night if I don't know all the dirty details of who I'm working for. You know, money is money, right? Bad people are going to get certain things anyway, so why shouldn't I earn a few dollars helping them? At least I'm not a total piece of trash, and I won't use my personal money to hurt people, so really I'm kind of laundering their money from bad purposes to neutral." She nodded with a satisfied smile.

Shay remained silent, her mouth pressed into a thin line.

"You still haven't explained why I should give a shit." James folded his arms. "I don't rescue people from their own mistakes without a good reason, and you sound like a piece of shit."

Harper gasped. "That's so unfair, James. I'm not a bad person. I'm just not a good person. And this isn't just about me. The artifacts I lost could hurt innocent people. Don't you care about them?"

"All the more reason to call the PDA."

"The Southguards have contacts in the government. I don't even know who I could trust. If we get them involved, there's no guarantee Southguard agents won't collect those artifacts before the PDA shows up, so then I die, the bad guys get the goods, and innocent people are still hurt. That's lose-lose for Team Cute Courier."

"I so want to stab you in the eye right now," Shay muttered.

"Hormones, am I right?"

"How do you go through life not getting slapped every five minutes?" Shay asked.

"Oh, don't be a hater." Harper winked. "We hot chicks have to stick together."

James let a low, long growl. Thomas whimpered and ran upstairs.

"Now you made me scare my dog, and I'm trying to figure out why you're stupid enough to explain that you're a piece of shit, and why I should care if you die. I'm not a merc for hire, and I doubt these artifacts you lost are that big a deal."

Harper sighed. "They kind of are." She looked at Shay. "You're a professor who studies this kind of thing. You ever heard of the Seasons of Rage?"

Shay grimaced, then gasped. "You're shitting me. You were transporting *those*? Are you insane?"

"What are the Seasons of Rage?" James dropped his arms and creased his brow in worry. Shay being spooked wasn't a good sign.

"A series of different synergistically-interacting arti- facts." Shay pinched the bridge of her nose and took a deep breath. "I've only ever read the legends about them. They're Oriceran, from the Great War. They were lost after the end of the war. Individually, they aren't a big deal, but if you put all of them together, they basically produce a magical war factory. The legends say they can create an endless number of magical soldiers. Entire kingdoms have fallen to the artifact's creations."

Harper bobbed her head. "Yeppers. That's the deal, and they kind of are on and already making soldiers. I was attacked on-site by some generated soldiers after they acti- vated automatically when my dampening was disrupted. The only thing we have going for us is the lower level of magic on Earth and a few preparations by yours truly. Otherwise, you know, Texas would be kind of screwed."

James pointed at her hands. "Those rings are artifacts? Enough that you weren't afraid of our guns or Shay's knife."

Harper nodded and then tugged on the collar of her sweater. "This too."

"And you couldn't win?"

"Somehow, the stupid soldiers are adaptive." Harper

waved her hands in front of her chest. "I have no idea how it works, but for most of my artifacts, even my nullifiers failed pretty quickly." She threaded her fingers again, her eyes wide and her bottom lip out. "Come on, James. I need your help. If the Seasons find a way to tap into a kemana or something, it's going to start popping out serious trouble, and then it'll be a Great War starting in Texas. We don't have a lot of time. I've set up a few artifacts in the area to try to slow it, but it's only a matter of time before it adjusts to those as well."

Shit. Adaptive magic? That's even worse than what I have.

"Why didn't you just run and hide?" Shay asked, a curious look in her eyes. "The PDA and military would eventually get involved. The Seasons are powerful, but even if they're adaptive, they can be defeated. The Oricerans did it before. They were just too dumb to destroy them. Or too greedy."

"It's like I said earlier. I might not be a good person, but I'm not a bad person. I simply have a little moral flexibility. This is professionally embarrassing too, and I'm not going to let a bunch of people die while I go hide. Even I have my limits, and once I realized it was the Southguards, I couldn't bring myself to let them have it."

James shook his head. "But your moral flexibility means you still won't risk going to the PDA?"

"A girl's got to keep breathing, right? No offense. I don't want anyone else to die, but I don't want to either." Harper smiled, an almost playful joy in her eyes. "I just need you to be the muscle. I can kill the entire factory with the Eye of Winter, which is kind of the failsafe device. I can take it to the central core of the little base the Seasons have made and end this all, but there's no way I can make it there alive without your help. And before you say something like, 'Why not just give it to me?' this girl needs a little insurance. Since I'm kind of sort of doing the right thing, I don't want to end up in jail or dead. It doesn't seem fair."

"Yeah, this is all about being fair to the mercenary courier who almost delivered a magical war factory to an entire family of evil bastards." Shay leaned back, weariness on her face. "The plan is, James and you go to Texas. He kicks some magical soldier ass, and you kill the Seasons?"

"Easy-peasy," Harper replied with a nod. She pointed at James. "As long as I have him. We'll drive straight there. This will all be over in a couple of days, and the Lone Star state doesn't become a war zone."

James furrowed his brow. "I'm not a huge fan of flying, but if this is such a big deal, why not take a plane?"

"Evil rich guys with piles of cash and influence, remember?" Harper rolled her eyes. "Right now, some of those very much bad and not nice people are looking for me because they're wondering where their missing artifacts are, and they have a lot of money to throw at looking for me. If it weren't for my artifacts, I'd probably already be dead. If I show up at an airport, it'll be easier for them to potentially spot me."

"What about a portal?" Shay suggested.

"If I take off the artifacts that are stopping them from using magic, either from a rental wizard or an artifact, they might be able to track me, and then it's game over. If they get me, they'll also get the only halfway decent way to stop the Seasons without blowing up half of Texas once that thing really gets going, or they'll grab everything and do something dangerous with it later."

James pointed at Shay's stomach. "My wife is weeks away from giving birth. I don't have time for this shit."

"Even if it involves saving people's lives?" Harper batted her eyelashes.

Shay groaned. "Do that again in front of me, and I *will* stab you."

"Touchy."

"That said," Shay continued, "you should go, James."

"Huh?" He frowned. "You said no road trips."

She shook her head. "It'll be annoying if you have to leave in the middle of labor because the government needs you to stop an army of magical soldiers, or they declare martial law after dropping a nuke on Austin to stop the Seasons. If she's right and these really are the Seasons of Rage, this could get bad."

"And if she's wrong?" James asked.

Shay grinned. "Punt her through a window."

Harper made a gagging sound. "You two are so messed up." She stopped and sidled over to James, extending her hand. "How about it, James? I need you. Texas needs you. The country needs you. And maybe the planet needs you."

James shook her hand. "I'm only doing this because I don't want to have to worry about it later."

Harper clapped once. "Great! I would really suggest we keep this between the three of us. The more people we involve, the more danger there is to all of us. I've already taken extraordinary measures to get here without the Southguards tracking me down."

"One last road trip it is," James rumbled.

"Okay." Harper skipped to the door with a joyful smile. "I'll be back tomorrow morning."

"Tomorrow morning? Aren't we on the clock?"

"Yeah, but I've got to lay down a few more trails for the Southguards," Harper explained. "If they catch up with us, it'll end up being too complicated because they can bring a whole army of goons. They're sniffing closer than I would like, but I've got a nice, secure rental Toyota for the trip."

"A Toyota? Why aren't we taking my truck?"

"Because it's kind of famous. *Duh.*"

Harper gestured toward the door. "Every time you go somewhere, you make too much noise, so we're going to try to keep this on the down-low, okay?"

It made perfect sense once she said it, but he still didn't like the idea of taking a road trip in another vehicle. A quick job to beat down someone in his own city was one thing, but it almost felt like he was cheating on his truck.

"But I don't want to make a road-trip in a Toyota," James mumbled.

CHAPTER ELEVEN

S hay glanced at her watch. "Harper should be here in a few minutes."

James finished checking the pockets of another gray coat grabbed from the closet. There was plenty of ammo for the .45, along with more than enough Shay treats if he needed them. He didn't care about bringing anything but a single change of clothes. His plan was to drive straight through and finish the job as fast as possible.

"There's something I want you to have. Wait here." Shay disappeared into the bedroom and reappeared with a small clear rock. She held it out in the palm of her hand. "Take this."

James took the smooth rock and rubbed it between his thumb and forefinger. "What is it?"

"Single-use portal artifact. Swallow it, then focus on where you want to go, and it'll open the portal. The portal will stay in place for about ten seconds."

"Why do I need a portal?"

Shay glowered. "Because that woman, besides being

annoying as fuck, is trouble. The minute you've cleaned up her mess for her, I wouldn't be surprised if she tries to steal everything but your belt buckle and leave you for dead."

"I can handle trouble." James grunted. "And if she thinks she can win against me because of a few magical dampening artifacts, she can have a discussion in Hell with Jonathan about how that shit doesn't work on me."

Shay folded her arms and gave him a stern look. "I'm your very pregnant wife, and I demand that you take the damned portal stone. If this somehow goes badly, I don't want to have to go on a bloody vengeance spree right after giving birth. I haven't tried it before, but I can only imagine it's hard to shoot at people when you're breastfeeding."

"You could have Maria watch the kid while you get your revenge," James suggested. He lifted his hands at Shay's angry glare. "It's fine. I've got it. I'll use it if I need it." He tucked the artifact into a pocket.

A boring gray Toyota sedan pulled into the driveway. The tinted windows denied a look at Harper at the wheel. She honked twice.

Shay leaned in to give James a soft kiss. "Save the world. At least save Texas."

"I've got to save Texas. It'd hurt the barbeque world too much to lose them."

Harper drummed her fingers on the wheel as they joined a HOV lane on I-10 east. "Thanks, James. You're a real peach. I won't lie to you; I thought about just ducking out on all this, but that seems like a real bitch move."

"That's one way to describe it," James muttered. "Since we're taking a road trip and we're heading to Texas, we're going to grab some barbeque along the way. I can also drive a lot of the time. I have tools that make it so I don't need as much sleep."

He didn't want to explain that he could use Whispy to avoid fatigue. The less Harper knew about his true capabilities, the better.

"That's cool." Harper gave him a pained look. "But barbeque? Do we have to stop?"

James frowned. "Yeah. Need to eat, and I like barbeque."

"Everyone knows you like barbeque, James. I'm sure if there are aliens out there on some distant planet, they probably know it too, but I'm a vegan."

James barked a laugh.

Harper scoffed. "It's not *that* funny. I'm just saying. What am *I* supposed to eat?"

"If you hadn't been helping those evil fuckers smuggle a death factory, you wouldn't be on a barbeque-heavy road trip with me," James replied. "So I don't give two shits about your eating preferences. You convinced me to help, so I'm helping, but I'm not even getting paid for this, so the least you're gonna do is buy me barbeque. If you don't like it, eat some potatoes and salad and shit."

"Fine." Harper's easy smile returned. "You've got a point. I'm asking a lot of you, and I do owe you."

"I'm glad you understand because I want to make this very clear. I'm only doing this because there are a lot of lives on the line and my wife told me to do it. Once this is over, I better never, ever see you again if you want to keep breathing. I don't like people complicating my life with their fuck-ups, especially when they happened because they got greedy."

Harper tucked a loose strand of hair behind her ear. The woman possessed a delicate beauty, but James barely noticed. He had Shay. He didn't need to look at any other women. Alison, as his daughter, didn't register the same way, and most of the women at the agency he just thought of as "one of the guys."

"You can't totally blame me, you know," the courier offered quietly. "I mean, it's not like I go out of my way to take jobs from evil dudes. Plenty of legitimate people hire me because of my particular specialty. It just so happens these were a nasty group of guys who wanted a nasty artifact."

"Listen to yourself." James scoffed. "Nothing's ever your fault, is it?"

"Oh, come on." Harper offered him a playful grin. "I get that you're the Barbeque Ghost now instead of the Granite Ghost, but are you trying to tell me you've never taken a job that was questionable?"

"I hunted bounties," James replied, looking out the window at the dense traffic in the other lanes. "I still do on occasion. If I go after someone, it's because they've done something to earn a bounty, or they fucked with me or people I care about. That means they brought it on themselves."

"It must be wonderful to be so perfect," Harper replied, a hint of mockery in her voice.

"I'm not perfect. I'm a sinner. That's why I go to church."

Harper laughed. "Oh, come on. Let me talk about it

another way. Not all bounties are horrible people, right? Maybe someone got framed, but you went after them. Some poor schlep who is afraid, and the next thing, James Brownstone's shooting him in the knee. You telling me that never happened?"

"I took on jobs with full knowledge of what was involved." James shrugged. "If I ran into someone and I had some reason to let them go, I did it with full knowledge of the implications, and I made sure to keep them in check if I thought they were dangerous. The few times I took on a blind job and it ended complicated, it wasn't because the people who hired me were the trouble. It was because someone else didn't know when to back the fuck off." He frowned at her. "Taking on a blind job like you did involving such a dangerous artifact makes you stupid, and for all I know, you've carried some artifact for dangerous fuckers who've hurt people before. If you want to convince me we're the same, give it up. If you want absolution, talk to a priest."

Harper sighed. "You're a barrel of laughs. I don't understand how you landed such a hot wife. Fine, James. Let's just get to Texas and take care of the Seasons, then you never have to see me again."

CHAPTER TWELVE

James pulled the car into the parking lot of the Bobby-Q BBQ Restaurant and Steakhouse in Phoenix. They'd switched drivers about two hours prior, at his suggestion. The less direct control Harper had, the more comfortable he felt, especially since he wasn't about to spend the entire time bonded to Whispy. The symbiont didn't always shut up when it would be good for him to, and he didn't want to listen to hours of requests for him to murder Harper.

The woman wrinkled her nose. "I can't believe you're making me eat at a steakhouse. This is almost cruel."

"Life sucks, you accidentally release a dangerous artifact, then you die," James replied. He nodded at the dashboard clock. "It's a little past noon, and we're making good time. Let's just eat and get out of here. According to the last message I got from my people, they can't get a decent direct satellite image of the place, but there are a lot of weird energy readings, even if they're contained in a small area."

"That's good. I'm using up a lot of expensive, limited artifacts to keep the Seasons in check. I'm glad they weren't a total waste. One thing, though." Harper placed her arm on his shoulder. She withdrew it at his glare. "We didn't bring your truck along to draw attention, and people can't see into the car well enough to tell it's you when we're driving. If you march into a barbeque place looking like you, people will take pictures, and if the Southguards figure out you might be involved with this at all, they'll have an arrow pointing toward the Seasons. Besides all their artifacts, they have mercenary wizards on their payroll."

James shrugged. "I can call in an order, and you can go in there and pick it up."

"And deal with that smell in the car for the next few hours? No, thank you." Harper reached into the back seat and pulled out a fedora. She handed it to James. "Put this on. It'll disguise you."

"Just putting on a hat isn't much of a disguise." He took the hat and turned it over a few times. It was a gray felt fedora. There was nothing special about it that he could tell.

"Glasses were good enough for Superman," Harper countered with a chuckle. "And it's not just a hat. It's an artifact. It'll make you look plain. It'll even fool cameras." She unbuttoned her sweater and tossed it on the floor. She was wearing a tight pink T-Shirt for the band Atlantis and Doom underneath. "I'm hoping nobody attacks us in there; if so, I'm really going to regret leaving that thing in here. If I can drop my enchanted sweater, you can put on the hat."

"Why not just wear the sweater?" James asked.

Harper pointed to the temperature readout on the dash: one hundred degrees. "I think people will kind of question why I'm wearing a sweater in Phoenix in June. I'm ditching my sweater, and you're putting that hat on."

James grumbled but slipped on the hat. His body shimmered for a moment, then his coat, shirt, and pants vanished, along with the hat. They were replaced by a white button-up shirt and blue slacks. His tattoos were gone. He looked into the rearview mirror. His face was subtly altered. If he squinted, he still could see the resemblance, but Harper had been right. It was like every distinguishing feature had been replaced by something more generic, like he was twenty different men averaged together.

"It'll wear off in an hour, so we need to be in and out by then," Harper explained.

"Fine," James replied. "Let's get some food."

Neither James nor Harper spoke more than a few words to each other for the next fifteen minutes. Their discussion with the waiter lasted longer. Conversations flowed around them, mostly about mundane work, sports, and entertainment. They sipped their waters, each watching the other, James with a scowl on his face, Harper with a soft smile.

I hate how she's always smiling like she knows what's going on. Like everything's a big joke to her.

She reached into her pocket, pulled out a small silver cube, and set it on the edge of the table. "If you're worried about being overheard, this will take care of it. It filters out sound, and this version even feeds false sound outside. If people are listening, they'll overhear a slightly strange conversation about the weather."

James's gaze traveled from the cube to the woman. "You're ex-CIA?" He stopped himself before he asked if she had worked as an alien hunter. The silence cube technology wasn't necessarily limited to that division of the CIA. It just so happened he'd almost exclusively had contact with them.

"Me?" Harper laughed and shook her head. "I wouldn't last a day working for the CIA. No, I was dating a guy for a while who worked for the CIA. He gave me this one day, disappeared, and told me never to look for him." She shrugged. "Spies! What are you going to do, right?"

"You do realize he's probably dead."

She doesn't look old enough to have been dating anyone when Fortis was still around, but who knows?

Harper picked up her water and took a sip. "We're not all James Brownstone. If he told me to stay away, I'm assuming he knew what he was talking about. I was going to break up with him in a few weeks anyway, so it was convenient. Win-win, you know? Well, for me, at least."

James scoffed. "You really don't care about anyone but yourself, do you?"

"If that were true, I wouldn't be on this trip with you." Harper looked to the side as the waiter approached. He set down a tray of ribs for James and a baked potato for her. She thanked him and touched his arm with a smile. The waiter smiled back.

James picked up a rib and took a bite, savoring the

play of the sauce on this tongue and the fact that it came from a normal four-legged cow that didn't taste like pineapple dipped in sugar. He polished off three ribs before speaking. "I'm still not totally convinced I shouldn't call the PDA or FBI on your ass. I'd check for bounties, but I'm sure Harper isn't your real name, and I don't want to trip some system looking for you. I don't need the Southguards blowing up the car on the highway."

"Harper *is* my real first name," she replied. "I'm not about to give you my real last name, but I can tell you there are no bounties on me. As for turning me in, I know how to work the Eye of Winter. Will your PDA agents know how to use it?"

James frowned. "If you care about other people getting hurt, wouldn't you be willing to tell them anyway, even if you were in jail?"

Harper rolled her eyes and smirked. "Of course not. That'd be stupid, right? A girl needs to have a backup plan. Besides, I'm trying to do the right thing here. Don't make it too hard on me."

James grunted and picked up a fresh rib. "You only have to do the right thing because of your previous screwup while you were in the process of doing the wrong thing."

"So judgmental." Harper plopped in a forkful of potato into her mouth. "Probably because you eat all that beef." She winked.

Does she really think she can flirt with me to get me to change my opinion?

"Yeah, keep telling yourself that, Rabbit Girl," James replied. "I thought you had moral limits, but apparently, you'll throw thousands of people aside as long as it means you don't end up in jail."

"Jail?" Harper blew a raspberry. "Jail I could handle, but this isn't just about me screwing up some courier work. This is about me trafficking in high-level illegal artifacts. The government might even classify the thing as a Broken Wand." She grimaced. "Oh, man. Now I feel bad. Just like that thing in LA, back in the day. Were you in the city when that happened? I was still a teen back then, but I was thousands of miles away."

"Yeah, I was there." James allowed himself a slight smile. He didn't care that people didn't know the truth about the Battle of LA. He knew he'd stopped the Vax, and that was enough.

Harper downed some more water before continuing. She shook her fork at James like a weapon. "The point is if the PDA or FBI arrests me, I'm not going to end up in county lockup for six months. I'm going to end up in an ultramax, or maybe even a place like Trevilsom. The Oricerans don't take kindly to people trafficking in Great War artifacts."

"You're too dangerous," James muttered before returning to his rib. "But fine. I need you for now."

I can't let this woman go. She's gonna lose a magical nuke for the North Koreans next month.

The woman watched him for a moment, her lips parted and a playful gleam in her eyes.

"What?" James rumbled. He set his rib down. "Staring makes the food taste bad."

"How about a magic trick?" Harper asked. She set down

her utensil and waved her hands. "Magic," she whispered dramatically.

"What the fuck are you going on about now?"

The corners of her mouth turned up in a grin. "It's an impressive trick." She picked up the fork and placed the tines against her head. "I'm going to use the metal in this as a telepathic antenna to reveal your thoughts."

"Good luck." James grabbed his rib. Quality barbeque was going cold while he wasted time listening to this woman's bullshit.

"I'm going to turn in that hot bitch the minute this is all over," Harper offered in a low voice, a sad attempt at imitating James' speech. "I want to turn her in now, but I can't because she has the Eye, so once the Seasons are disabled, I'll knock her out, hogtie her, and deliver her to the nearest PDA or FBI field office."

James snorted. "'Hogtie?' I'm from LA. We don't say 'hogtie.'"

Harper laughed. "Same idea. Tell me I'm wrong."

He shrugged. "We all have to pay for our mistakes eventually."

"It's okay." Harper lowered her fork to gather more potato. "I know that's probably been your plan from the beginning, and I'm telling you this to prove I'm not the totally sociopathic bitch you think I am. For me, the plan is as follows. I'm going to use you as my meat shield. I'm going to go disable the Seasons, and then I'm going to skip out before you even know what's going on. I'll hide on some tropical island until the Southguards forget about me."

James chuckled. "That's your plan?"

"I've got a lot of money and artifacts stashed around." Harper made a large circle in the air with her fork. "I could hide out for a few years."

"It won't work. I've heard this plan before. You want me to do a magic trick and tell you the future?"

Harper grinned. "A joke? You're threatening to develop a personality, James. What do you see in my future? Me scrubbing toilets in an ultramax?"

"Nah." James shook his head. "You convince yourself you don't care about anyone, and you decide to go to that island. Maybe you fake your death first, decide to do a few other jobs in a different field. You end up making a few friends, including one who dedicates himself to making great pizza. Maybe an apprentice, too, and the next thing you know, you end up settling down with some guy and turning your back on your past. You retire to something that doesn't involve dangerous magic at all."

Harper blinked a few times. "Okay. That's oddly specific, but at least it isn't prison." She tapped her watch. "Remember, we're on the clock before your disguise wears off. That hat takes two hours to recharge for every hour you wear it."

"Don't worry. I'll be done in ten."

She's not a total waste of space. She is right. If she does have money, she could have just said fuck it and run. Maybe there is hope for her yet, but I'm not gonna let my guard down.

CHAPTER THIRTEEN

By the time James and Harper made an early evening stop at Borderland BBQ in Las Cruces, the whole road trip experience almost felt like a careful routine, complete with disguise hat and silence cube. He reached into his pocket to pull out an energy potion after a long yawn. He downed the potion before preparing to chow down on some brisket. Harper continued her transformation into a rabbit with a salad. At least a potato was defensible food for a grown human.

Harper eyed the empty vial as James slipped it back into his pocket. "That's your brilliant plan for staying awake? A potion? You could have just let me drive more instead of nap. Or taken a pill."

"That's just to get me there. Once we're on-site, I've got a few other tricks," James took a bite of his brisket. "It's not a big deal, anyway. I've got a witch who makes them for me in bulk."

"Aren't we fancy?" Harper chuckled.

"Maybe." James chewed for a moment and swallowed. "There's something I've been meaning to ask you."

"Go ahead." Harper shrugged. "You can ask whatever you want. I'm not saying I'll answer, or tell you the truth, but I'm not going to care if you ask. I'm very hard to offend, unlike you."

"I'm not easy to offend. Most people are just annoying."

"Sure, sure," Harper replied.

"You said you used to be a tomb raider," James stated. He took another bite of brisket, chewing carefully while he waited for the answer. Something poked at the back of his mind, propelling him to want to learn more about his temporary partner.

"That's not a question. That's a statement, but it's the truth. I was a tomb raider for three years, actually. I was the partner-slash-apprentice of a guy who'd been doing it a little longer than me." A wistful smile appeared. "He wasn't a bad guy, actually, but tomb raiding isn't safe. He ended up dead. I didn't. Plenty of stories end that way. I imagine it's not all that different in bounty hunting. You've lost people."

"Yeah. I have, and I think about them all the time." James stared at her. "But I'm not you. Did you leave him to die?"

Harper's omnipresent smile vanished. Her eyes grew stormy, and her mouth twitched. The crack in the persona was ephemeral as a new grin displaced her frown. "If he got killed, it's his own fault for not being careful, right? He was the guy who was supposed to know what he was doing."

James snorted. "You were genuinely pissed there. I struck a nerve, which means you actually gave a shit about that guy. Why are you so hell-bent on pretending like you don't give a shit?"

"Just because I'm looking out for myself doesn't mean I don't care about anyone else," Harper explained. "So, yeah, you win." She threw up her hands in mock surrender. "I did care about him, and for the record, no, I didn't leave him to die. If you have to know, he died saving me from a trap." She gestured to her face and then her body. "Then again, what man wouldn't die to save all this, right? It's a net win for the universe."

"Is that why you quit being a tomb raider?" James asked. He didn't need to be a psychiatrist to see the obvious defense mechanism.

"Why did you quit being a bounty hunter?" Harper countered.

"I didn't. I still do the occasional bounty."

Harper rolled her eyes. "Oh, come on. You've even said publicly that you're semi-retired."

"I suppose family was a big reason I stopped," James admitted.

"You didn't stop when you adopted Alison."

"It took a few years for me to absorb it all. I had something else I cared about, and that made me care less about bounty hunting. I haven't needed the money in a while, so I only do the occasional hunt to keep my skills up. Alison went into security because she wants to help protect people, and it's a way she can do that without too many restrictions."

Why the fuck am I telling her all this?

Harper gasped. "It's weird. Spooky, even. I just thought of something." She pointed at him. "I'm around her age.

There could be some sort of timeline where I end up as Harper Brownstone." She giggled. "Can I call you Dad?"

"If you do that, I will call up the Southguards myself and turn you over," James growled.

"Oh, you're no fun." Harper stuck out her tongue. "Loosen up, James."

James grunted. "Yeah, and I doubt that shit you said anyway. It's not like Alison had a fun time getting to that point. She suffered a lot. Is that your deal? You get fucked over by a parent? End up an orphan or something? That's your excuse for not giving a fuck?"

"Nope. Not at all. My life was spoiled and easy-peasy," Harper related. She munched the bite off her fork. "If anything, my parents were too loving. They don't know about my careers, of course. I've told them I'm a personal shopper for this rich businessman in Singapore, which is why I have to travel all over the world. But Alison? I know about all that stuff your daughter went through. I saw the movie, the one with that one actress. You know, what's-'er-name."

James shrugged. Several different movies had been made about Alison's adoption, all unauthorized, and all of which took liberties with reality. He was particularly annoyed with one that implied he had been in a relationship with Alison's mother before meeting her, the implication being, Alison was secretly his biological daughter.

Harper set her fork down and folded her hands, then set her elbows on the table and rested her chin on her hands with an amused expression. "I don't have a sad story of abuse or poverty, James. My parents were rich and kind, and I could have cruised through life pretty easily without a want in the world. I ended up with that tomb raider because my life felt empty. I tried charity like my mother, and I tried a few internships to satisfy my father, but I wanted something more, and things never felt more alive than when I was risking my life. I did some extreme sports, but that seemed pointless. I found out pretty quickly that I needed a real goal for it to mean something. I need risk plus reward. That was the formula."

"And you quit being a tomb raider after the guy died? That finally shock you and make you realize it wasn't a game?"

"Life's a game, James. Everyone agrees it is. They just disagree on how we should keep score." Harper shook her head. "And, no, I didn't want to quit after that. I did it for another year, actually, but then I realized something important. I liked the thrill of it all, but I hated the caves and nastiness associated with it. When I was with him, I didn't mind as much, but once he was gone, it became obvious. I mean, no surprise. It's tomb raiding, not spa raiding, right?"

James scoffed. "Yeah. So you switched over to being a courier?"

"It was surprisingly easy." Harper tapped her forehead. "Especially when you're as smart as I am. I already had the relevant contacts from my tomb-raiding days, so it was just a matter of putting out a new shingle. It took me a couple of years, but I ended up with a decent rep, and everything was going along well until this annoying little incident." She sighed. "Such is life." She clucked her tongue. "But this will all be a nasty bump in the past soon enough, and I can go back to being fabulously cute and awesomely talented."

"You know what all this tells me?" James stared at her, watching her expression carefully.

"That I'm awesome, and you should worship my beauty and talent?" Harper grinned. Any hint of the introspective woman was gone, replaced by the mask.

"That's just the point. You *are* talented. Talented enough to survive as a tomb raider and a high-value courier." James pointed to the top of his head. "To think ahead about disguises." He nodded at the cube. "And how to keep yourself from being spied on. You were brave enough to break into my house. This means you're not a total piece of shit, and you could do something halfway worthwhile with your life instead of being an errand girl for criminals."

Harper rolled her eyes. "Not all my clients are criminals. Just…some."

"You don't even verify most of your clients, so how the hell do you even know?"

Harper snorted. "What am I supposed to do? Go open a security company or become a college professor? Run a barbeque restaurant? I don't play well with others, James, and I don't like being tied down to one place. I know exactly what and who I am, and I'm going to continue to be that person. Don't think you can give me a few stories about loving your wife and daughter, and I'll repent and start attending church with you."

"I don't really give a shit either way. I'm just saying." James shrugged. "You're right. I have a restaurant now. I'm mainly helping you now because Shay convinced me, but even if we stop the Seasons, nothing will change if you don't change. You'll end up in this same situation six months from now, or two years from now. Someday. You'll bat your eyelashes, but no one will come and help you. The next thing you know, the people you thought were your friends are trying to kill you in your own house."

"Boring lecture, pseudo-Dad," Harper replied.

"What did I say about that?" His nostrils flared.

"You said I couldn't call you 'Dad,' so I called you something else." Harper smirked. "Looking out for number one isn't evil, or even selfish. It's pragmatic. Let's be real. That's all anyone in the world can do."

James shook his head. "I used to think that. I don't anymore. I have friends and people who actually give a shit about me. I have a family."

Harper offered a flirtatious wave to a man in a few tables down. "Is this all because your wife is about to pop?"

"I don't know. Maybe."

James forked up another piece of brisket. He wasn't sure. The whole thing might be a combination, perhaps, of what had happened with Calista and the fact Harper was so young. She wasn't totally wrong. Something about the courier vaguely reminded him of his daughter, a talented young woman in a dangerous field. It just seemed like a waste, just as it had with Trey and his boys.

There was potential there, but it wasn't his responsibility. She wasn't a child, and unlike Trey, Alison, and many others he'd helped, she didn't have an excuse other than selfishness.

She chose her life, and now other people are suffering for her mistakes.

"Don't worry about it," James rumbled, the souring mood muting his enjoyment of the brisket. "Let's just finish and get out of here."

CHAPTER FOURTEEN

James rolled to a stop and pulled off the highway onto the shoulder. "This is it?" He peered into the dark forest. A faint shadow of a hump stood in the distance—Granite Mountain if the map had been right. It was hard for a Californian like him to consider it a true mountain. The night was clear, but they were in the middle of nowhere, only the dim glow of a nearby town helping push away near-complete darkness.

"I didn't tell you to stop because I needed to go the bathroom," Harper answered, rolling her eyes. "Yes, this is it."

"And you know where you're going?" he asked.

"You don't just lose something like that," Harper replied. She pointed. "We need to get the car off the road. We don't want any cops grabbing the car or investigating." She smirked. "Even if you think law enforcement should get involved, think about how dangerous it is. I'm here just to do my part to shut the Seasons down before they beat the containment and dampening artifacts."

He pulled forward, the car shaking as it moved off-road. "Too bad we don't have a nice big Ford *truck* about now." He slanted a glance at her.

Harper shrugged. "Trash the car if you want. It's not like I'm dropping this thing back off. I'm disappearing after all this is done. If the cops want to investigate the mysterious disappearance of the driver after this is over, all the better. They'll probably just assume I died when they find the remains of the Seasons' work."

"I'm not gonna knock you too much. It's not like I haven't trashed my share of rental cars in my day."

"See, pseudo-Dad? We're bonding!"

James let out a long grunt. "Every time I stop being annoyed with you for five seconds, you go out of your way to fix that."

"Words hurt."

"Magical death factories hurt."

Harper laughed. "They do, but this one won't very soon."

This hasn't been the best road trip, but at least the barbeque has been good, and this shit isn't even in my top ten of annoying jobs.

James continued for a few hundred feet, the forest assaulting the bottom and sides of the car. The trees soon grew too dense and forced him to stop. Driving through an unlit forest at night was pointless. They would end up wrapped around a tree. "We're hoofing it from here."

Harper reached into a backpack in the back and fished out some pearl cat-eye glasses. She slipped them on. "Ah, that will do it."

"What, you suddenly care about fashion? We're stopping some doom artifact here, not taking selfies for dating profiles." James sneered.

"We're close enough now, is why I got these out." Harper tapped the side of the glasses. "These let me see the magical emanations from the Seasons, despite them being mostly muted. We can walk straight toward them with my help." She opened the door. "Don't worry, pseudo-Dad. If all goes well, this will be over in a few hours, and you can go back to ignoring me because I'm not the daughter you always wanted."

"You're not my daughter."

"You could always adopt me." Harper batted her eyelashes.

"Let's just get this shit over with," James rumbled.

Harper saluted. She grabbed her backpack, stepped outside, and slammed the door, then donned the backpack and shook out her hands. "Ah, you have to love that crisp forest air."

James reached under his shirt to pull the spacer off his amulet. He hissed, the pain of Whispy's bonding pushing out the building fatigue from his lack of sleep.

Initiation, the symbiont sent. *What is the nature of the enemy?*

Don't know yet. They may be adaptive.

That suggests increased probability of symbiont adaptation, Whispy suggested, eagerness radiating from him. *Engage and kill enemies for maximum potential adaptation.*

I don't really know if we're going to be killing anything as much as breaking things, but we'll definitely have some enemies to fight.

James opened his door and stepped outside. He

squinted. "I can't see shit. I have my own tricks, but did you bring a flashlight?"

"Something better," Harper suggested. "Flashlights are boring." She tapped one of her rings and a glowing orb appeared a few feet above her, bathing the area in soft light. A few small, furry animals scurried away from the light.

"That works," James mumbled. He patted his coat down to confirm his Shay treats and magazines were still in there. It was likely to be a Whispy-intensive night, but if he could solve the problem with a few bullets, he would. "Lead on."

Harper skipped a few feet before settling into a normal walk. "It's just a few miles from here."

"It's a few miles off the highway?" James asked, surprise in his voice.

"Yep."

The light buzz of cicadas and the occasional rustle in the bushes revealed they were not alone, but insects and animals didn't concern James. There wasn't a natural animal on the planet that had a chance against him while he was bonded. Most wouldn't do well against him even when he didn't have the amulet.

Maybe I should fight a bear, he thought.

Little adaptation potential from potential engagement, Whispy reported.

It was an idle thought. Wait, a few miles from the highway?

"From what I saw on the maps, there are a lot of small towns around, and Austin's only about fifty miles away," James observed.

"You're correct," Harper replied, glancing at him with a

bemused smile. "What about it?"

"That's a lot of people very damned close to the Seasons, and as you just pointed out, we're only a few miles from the highway." James glanced into the woods. The light reflected off yellow eyes. Whatever animal owned the eyes bounded deeper into the undergrowth. "How the hell did you end up basically dropping a WMD near a major city with a straight path to it? There are millions of people in the greater Austin area. Do you have any idea how many barbeque restaurants there are around here?"

Harper snickered. "So if there were no barbeque restaurants, would it be okay?"

James hesitated for a moment before shrugging. "Of course not. I just don't get you. Behind all the bullshit games and fake smiles, there's a brain, so I'm just trying to see how it went so wrong. Usually, if you're smuggling something like this, you keep it away from major areas. Or were you taking it to Austin?"

Harper spread out her arms to her sides. She jumped over a few raised roots. "I was supposed to drop it off in Seattle."

"Seattle?" James scoffed. "You would have caused trouble for my daughter, then."

"You're really bumming me out, pseudo-Dad. It's not like I planned any of this." Harper lowered her arms. "This is probably the worst situation I've been in."

An owl fluttered overhead, ignoring the intruders and disappearing deeper into the forest.

"Most of the times I've helped transport a really dangerous artifact, they didn't risk flying it," James explained. "You put that thing in a plane, meaning you risked it dropping almost anywhere, and all that 'planes are safer than cars' shit only applies when they are big commercial planes, not whatever little glider you were flying."

Harper rubbed the back of her neck. "Ornithopter, actually."

"Wait. Isn't that…" James snorted in disgust. "You weren't even flying an actual plane. It wasn't just a mechanical failure like you claimed. You were using some flying artifact, then?" He scrubbed a hand down his face. "Aren't you the person who specializes in dampening artifacts?"

Harper raised a finger. "Got it in one. I'm still not sure why it failed, but I'm not a total idiot. I know how to use certain artifacts and still protect myself. I don't even know how to fly a regular plane. The only way I'm getting through the air is with an artifact, and I needed the speed for the job."

"I don't get it." James pointed at the sky, most of the stars hidden by the trees. "You were here, you crashed, the artifact gets activated. You spend some time setting up the defenses, and then what…you call AAA and headed to town and flew to LA in a real plane?"

"Nope. Not entirely." Harper shook her head. "I had a portal artifact. It was supposed to be short-range, but I combined it with an amplifying artifact I had to get it to open a portal to LA. Both artifacts died and turned into puddles of goo, but at least I didn't. I got my bearings, made a few calls, and sent a few messages to get certain things in motion and misdirect the Southguards, then I wandered over to your place, where we had our lovely chat, and I convinced you via your very pregnant wife to help me fix this problem."

James fell silent for a long while processing all the details. There were federal agents and bounty hunters trying to clean things up. Spies, and even the Fixer, but how many people were flying around in magical contraptions with deadly artifacts tucked into the back? It was almost a miracle a major city hadn't gone up in a magical mushroom cloud yet, but that didn't mean everyone had escaped unscathed. The destruction of the Seattle kemana was proof of just how many people a few bad magicals could kill when left unchecked.

"That was risky," he rumbled. "Everything about this was risky. How did you know when you left that the Seasons would stop pumping out an army? Millions of people might have already been dead."

"Because I know the capabilities of the artifacts I deployed." Harper gave him a bright smile. "I thought we already established that I was talented. One reason I'm not dead is that I've always got backup plans. I knew the containment and dampening artifacts would keep it under control for a few days, so even if I couldn't convince you right away, I'd have a margin of error to either keep working on you or figure something out."

"Or just run?" James asked.

"Maybe." Harper shrugged. "It doesn't matter. Plus, with the magical signature muted at a distance, certain people wouldn't come accidentally sniffing around and find it. It'd be safe from the Southguards and others. It's not like I gave them a detailed flight plan."

"'And others?'" James' mouth twitched. "You mean like

the PDA? You kept insisting it would take too long and risk too much to contact them, but it still sounds like you just wanted to cover your ass."

"Everything I said about the Southguards was true." Harper glanced around after a branch cracked under one of her ankle boots. "Just because it also happens to be of benefit to me, it doesn't make it a bad thing. It doesn't matter anyway. We're here now. I paid for your disgusting barbeque, and now we need to end this. We can go our merry ways afterward, and you can go back to your wife and new kid feeling like you made the world a better place. I can hide on my island and reflect on the error of my ways."

They lapsed into silence, the night's song in the forest soothing in its own way. Even Whispy remained quiet, a vague pensive sense leaking from the symbiont. The noise of the animals relaxed James. If the Seasons had really been out of control, he doubted the forest animals would be staying nearby. He'd visited far too many eerily silent forests in his life.

At least she didn't lose this shit in some already-haunted forest.

Harper hummed a happy song under her breath, her easy movements making it seem like she was on a jaunt at some corporate trust retreat.

"Why do I get the feeling there's something you're holding back?" James asked.

Harper winked. "Oh, pseudo-Dad, don't be so suspicious. As your pseudo-daughter, I'm disappointed you don't believe me. I've been very honest with you, haven't I? I told you from the beginning how I screwed up. I admitted that I don't have a sob story. I guarantee I haven't lied to you."

"You know one thing you learn when you're a bounty hunter?"

"How to shoot people who are running away?"

James grunted. "You learn the best lies are surrounded by truth, and it's easy to leave something out if you shove a bunch of information at people. As far as I'm concerned, if you told me the ocean was full of water, I'd go to the beach to check. There's an angle here I'm still not seeing, and I'm going to remain on guard."

"That makes you smart." Harper slowed and squinted. She pushed the glasses up. "You can see it, right?"

A faint blue glow haunted the forest in the distance.

"Yeah." James nodded. "I can see it."

"Then let's hurry. I want to finish this up and go take a shower." Harper jogged toward the light.

James followed. The light grew closer and closer until it resolved into a glowing wall of energy surrounding a hole in the ground. A group of roughly bipedal humanoids made up of angular white material circled the hole. Several holes in the bodies revealed they were mostly hollow, with a pulsing blue glow within the central chest cavity. They lacked eyes, but the soft ochre glow from one side suggested something approaching a face. Four sharp fingers protruded from their long arms, the same glow emanating from them.

Harper drew a hollow bone rod from the backpack with a forced grin on her face. "Now's the rough part, pseudo-Dad."

James cracked his knuckles. "Yeah, it's time to go."

CHAPTER FIFTEEN

Harper licked her lips, lingering uncertainty on her face. She raised the bone rod. "Once I drop this field, it'll take me a little to get it back again. It's part of the dampening system. I can't predict what will happen, other than we'll probably get jumped. These guys are tough. I used up most of my defensive artifacts not getting shredded by them last time."

Let's start out at advanced mode, James thought.

"One second," James replied, shrugging off his coat. No reason to risk losing his gun, magazines, and Shay treats later. As Harper watched with open curiosity, James reached into his pocket and pulled out a small goddess figurine. He slipped it under his shirt and pressed it against the amulet. The artifact crumbled to dust, and James' armor covered most of his body seconds later. He extended a single blade. "Now I'm ready. Do we have a plan other than destroying every last one?"

Engage and kill enemies for maximum adaptation, Whispy

shouted in James' mind, rare excitement emanating from the symbiont.

"That sounds about right," Harper suggested. "The famous magic armor." She twirled the bone rod like a baton. "I'd love to see if any of my dampeners would work on it, but I'm guessing I'm not the first person to get that idea. Since you're still around, I doubt it would even work. I'm going to leave this to you, pseudo-Dad, because if it starts getting out of hand, I'm going to need to concentrate on trying to reestablish the barrier, so we survive and the nearby towns don't get overrun."

James grunted. "Fine. I'm ready. Drop it. The sooner we end this, the quicker I get to go home and take a few days off after this crap."

Harper raised the rod and made several precise movements in the air. She began chanting in a rhythmic fashion, her pitch rising and falling. James wasn't sure about the language, but he had heard Shay often enough to know Harper was likely speaking Enochian mixed with Old Aramaic. The tempo of her words increased, along with the speed of her movements. A glow suffused the rod and it buzzed softly. It grew in volume until a loud crack sounded and writhing, jagged lines of energy blasted from the rod and struck the blue field consuming it.

The artificial soldiers all turned and raised their arms. The brightness of their faces and chests increased.

"We've got their attention," James muttered.

Destroy enemies, destroy enemies, destroy enemies, Whispy chanted. He was more excited than James had felt in a long time.

James hunched and prepared to meet the charge of the

magical soldiers, but his opponents didn't charge. Instead, they spread out, forming two inverted Vs, their movements cautious and precise like a carefully choreographed marching band—one that happened to be made up of killer magical creations with claws. "Formations and tactics? I was expecting something a little more mindless zombie."

Harper wiped the sweat off her forehead as she took short, shallow breaths. "They might be artificial, but they're made using magic. They're not robots, and you can't think of them that way. They can act smarter than you would think. There's probably someone at a magic school some-where doing something weirder, like making self-aware cupcakes into an army."

James scoffed. That sounded like the kind of annoying shit that happened at places like the School of Necessary Magic, but the wider the gates to Oriceran opened, the more that kind of bizarre twisting of reality would become the norm on Earth. Fighting an old magical automaton factory might be nowhere near as bizarre as the kinds of challenges the planet would face in the coming centuries.

I can't worry about that. All I can do is take down the enemies in front of me.

"If they're smart, I guess I'll have to invert the expecta-tions." James bellowed a challenge, bringing up his blade. "Come on, assholes. We're here to destroy the Seasons of Rage. If you don't take us down, your little invasion is going to end before it began." He pointed the blade and slowly swept it through the air to point at different soldiers. "The Earth and Texas barbeque will be safe from your Oriceran pineapple magic-cow bullshit."

Harper crept toward a tree. "Pineapple magic cows?" she murmured.

The soldiers didn't move. Several crouched, their long, jointed legs at what would be uncomfortable angles for a human.

They might be smart, but it doesn't look like I can provoke them.

Engage and kill enemy immediately, Whispy demanded.

The symbiont had a point. With the containment field down, the clock was ticking faster than before.

James shrugged and charged one of the V formations. Once he had closed to within a few yards, the first formation broke apart, the soldiers rushing to surround him. He continued pushing forward and slammed his blade through the chest of a magical soldier. Its ochre and blue glow died, and the magical enemy collapsed to the ground and disintegrated into thick gray smoke. There were no screams or sounds other than the light thud of the body on the ground before its destruction.

"They're not so tough," James yelled.

Harper didn't respond. She reached into her backpack, but the surge of the rest of the formation focused James' attention on the soldiers. They swung their claws, and the first few blows ripped deep gouges in the armor. One dug into his side, drawing blood. The wound throbbed.

Yesssss, Whispy sent. *Adaptation in progress.*

James hissed and slammed his armored elbow into the attacker. The enemy flew backward and crashed into several others, taking them down. They scrambled to their feet.

He growled and sliced the head off another soldier, but

it kept up its attack. It was slower than before, but it didn't have any trouble striking him. Adding a new hole through its chest finished it. He backhanded and kicked a few others to give himself some space. They crashed to the ground, but they were on their feet in seconds. There was no sign they felt pain, fear, or worry. He couldn't intimidate them into surrender. He could only annihilate them.

The second V formation formed two looser circles around James. Individuals moving to fill the holes in the internal ring as the magical soldiers continued ripping at James' armor. They continued their shredding for a few more seconds before their blows began to bounce off instead of penetrating. The throbbing from James' side faded.

Moderate adaptation achieved, Whispy announced. *Regeneration in progress.*

Good. Those were decent hits. It's been a while.

As if testing James, the surrounding enemies stopped their attacks and made quick, careful swipes at different parts of his body. A few tried for his head, but perished for their attempts without landing a hit when he stabbed them. New silver-green metallic tendrils sprouted to fill and repair the damaged armor.

The careful testing ended when the entire remaining group of magical soldiers surged forward at once, ripping at him with no obvious tactics or target. Their claws scraped all parts of his armor but left only the shallowest of scratches in the regenerating surface layer.

You had your chance, assholes. Too late.

James punched a few of the enemy away before delivering a series of quick stabs to destroy the closest opponents. The thick cloud of smoke from the disintegrating bodies blinded him for a few seconds, allowing one opponent to claw at his unarmored face; the attack stung and drew blood. He sliced the soldier into three pieces, and it soon added its smoke to the cloud.

High adaptation achieved to existing attack type, Whispy reported. *Continued regeneration in progress.*

A bright flash ripped through the forest. A crackling white orb exploded against several soldiers trying to crawl over each other and claw James. The force of the attack scattered the magical soldiers, but they hopped to their feet in an instant, showing no permanent damage. James took his opportunity to push out of the hole and ripped through a few of his foes along the way. The soldiers attempted to regroup into something approaching a rough semi-circle, but now, free of the smoke and the constant attack, James became a machine, stabbing with brutal regularity to destroy foe after foe. Their lines thinned.

In the corner of James' eye, Harper held a sapphire pendant in front of her in her left hand and murmured something under her breath. Another crackling white orb blasted from the pendant and scattered more of the soldiers. A group turned toward her after standing back up. James leapt into their midst to stab their energy hearts, as he'd come to think of them. The enemy forces had been reduced to one-third of their original strength.

The survivors backed away from James, forming a tight line this time, their claws raised in front of them. Much of the earlier damage to his armor had already been repaired, and the cut on his face was gone.

"Are they afraid?" James wondered aloud. "Do they

realize I'm beating their asses and they aren't accomplishing anything?"

"I have no idea." Harper offered him a merry smile. "Before I was saying they were smart, but that's not the same thing as being self-aware. I just wanted you to not expect zombies. Not that it might have made a difference. Let's just finish them off. The longer we take, the more that might come. Remember, this thing is a factory, and I'm surprised there aren't more here."

"Ending this is fine by me." James crouched, jumped into the enemy line, and destroyed three of the enemies before they adopted a new triangular formation. The adjustment accomplished little as he continued ripping into the magical soldiers, his blade cutting through their bodies with ease. He punctured the last standing enemy before waving some of the now-thick acrid smoke out of his face and looking over at Harper. "I thought you weren't helping fight?"

He wasn't certain he needed the help, but that didn't kill his surprise.

Harper clipped the pendant around her neck and gave him a dismissive shrug and smile. "I'm committed to ending this now, and you looked like you were getting swarmed. Those guys were carving you up like a bunch of starving cats going after the same fish.

"I was okay, but thanks." James marched over to the hole and peered down. It was a ten-foot drop into a wide, roughly circular tunnel. Soft ochre light the same shade as the soldiers dimly illuminated the tunnel. There were no ramp or handholds. He wondered about the climbing and jumping capabilities of the magical soldiers. If they were smart enough to use formations, they were smart enough to get in and out of the hole efficiently.

Moderate potential for additional adaptation, Whispy reported. *Recommend additional engagement of enemies. Proceed into enemy base.*

"You said these things are adaptive," James commented. He gestured to the lingering clouds of smoke. "They got in a few good hits, but they didn't seem very tough afterward." He shrugged, a little surprised by his disappointment. Maybe he was becoming more like Whispy than Whispy was him.

"That might change in the future, but I don't know with you." Harper patted her pendant. "I destroyed several of them with this when I was leaving, but soon I was just bouncing them around and couldn't finish them." She eyed his blade with a greedy smile. "I'm surprised you were able to keep destroying them, but that was why I went to you for help. When you absolutely need something destroyed, go get James Brownstone. Maybe they can't adapt to whatever is powering your blade." She gestured to the hole. "Pitmasters first. Ladies second."

"Brave to the end, huh?"

"I'm here, aren't I?"

James dropped into the hole with a grunt and looked around for new enemies. There were no soldiers, but six different tunnels were evenly spaced around the entrance. Now that he was inside, he could see residual claw marks in the uneven tunnel walls.

Harper followed him in, her arms held to her sides at a slight angle. Her boots buzzed for a few seconds, and her fall slowed for the last few feet. She floated down the final three inches and bowed. "That's what I call an elegant fall."

She'd be nothing without her artifacts. Shay used a lot of toys in her day, but she kicks ass without them.

"Let's skip the elegance and finish destroying this thing," James replied. "I'm guessing since you disabled that barrier, this thing is going to rev up to a higher pace?"

"I would assume so, based on what I know." Harper shrugged, an apologetic smile on her face. "Omelets. Eggs. Right?"

"In this situation, I'm pretty sure we're the eggs." James looked around. The tunnels all looked the same to him, and there were no markings on the walls. "Where to? You're the woman with all the answers."

"Have faith, pseudo-Dad." She pulled out a white crystal on a chain. Elaborate curly script in a language James didn't recognize was etched in connected circular lines all around the crystal. She held up the chain and sang a short, odd melody. The crystal swung back and forth a few times before settling, the bottom raised and pointing toward one of the tunnels. "That way. Once we find the core, I'm going to need a good minute or two to complete the disarming sequence. If I go down, I suggest you run and call in the PDA and Army. I won't care because I'll be dead." Her irrepressible grin remained.

Harper motioned to the tunnel. "Pitmasters first."

CHAPTER SIXTEEN

James assumed once they entered the tunnels, it would be a simple matter of walking a few hundred yards and arriving at the core, but every twenty to thirty yards, they arrived at a new intersection with six tunnels, including their original one. Calling it a maze didn't adequately describe the interlocking complexity of the Seasons of Rage base the artifacts had dug underneath a Central Texas forest.

At this point, I don't even know if dropping a nuke on this would work. They'd have to drop several.

"I don't get this," he muttered. "Why is it so fucking complicated? It's just supposed to be a soldier factory, right?"

"Really? It makes perfect sense to me." Harper shrugged, a faint hint of disappointment on her face.

"How do you figure? What am I missing?"

"It's *not* just a soldier factory. It's an all-in-one invasion kit." Harper ran her free hand along a cave wall. "And if you make it this ridiculous maze, that means short of blowing the whole thing to hell with a huge blast, you're going to have to go through this place tunnel by tunnel to clear it out, all while it's making new reinforcements. I don't know all the particulars of this place, but there's a lot of magical reinforcement, too. It would be harder than you would think to just blow through from the top, and depending on where it's set up, that could cause problems. Think about it, though; this was built in days while being somewhat dampened. If it'd been going full speed, we'd already have a full war on our hands."

"You're telling me they purposely designed this shit to be as annoying as possible? As some sort of defensive strategy?"

"That's what I'd assume. The Oriceran Great War makes our world wars look like nothing." Harper related the idea with the casual excitement one might use for discussing of a summer movie. "It's like boom; America nukes Japan, and no one uses nukes again. It's been a hundred years and they still haven't. And nukes don't even blow up entire countries. The Oricerans *were* blowing away entire countries and stuff, right? You would know better than I would, given your wife's into that kind of thing. But you have to figure if they were scared enough that the treaty held for thousands of years, they must have made some of the most dangerous and nastiest things we could possibly imagine." She glanced at her tracking crystal and kept moving down the tunnel. "Something like that would be crazy-nasty. I mean, if you're a real jerk, you drop this into a populated area, and now your side has to go through these tunnels one by one, or you have to risk blowing the whole thing up before it really gets rolling, right? It's a good counter to them just dropping a magical nuke. If they made it just a big hole with guys streaming out, you just send a bunch of elf knights or something to mow them down and head straight to the core."

James grunted. "I hadn't thought of it that way."

Autonomous adaptive invasion forcing strategic limitations demonstrates excellent invasion potential, Whispy sent, admiration flavoring his thoughts.

Of course, you *appreciate it. These guys aren't pound-for-pound as tough as a bonded Vax, but they don't need to be. Quantity over quality.*

James scoffed, not as happy with the idea as his symbiont. "The Oricerans think they're so much better than us, but they have all these super-weapons they made and then had to hide after they almost destroyed their planet. My daughter had to fight some giant monster in Seattle they had used in the war. Sometimes I wonder if shit like that's gonna happen when the gates open wider. They still have their treaty, but we're only barely holding on."

"I read about that thing in Seattle. Crazy. She's a tough chick, but I suppose that's not a big surprise. Even if she's adopted, she's still a Brownstone." Harper paused to verify their course as they entered a new intersection. "But I don't think it's going to be the same thing here, no matter how wide the gates open. I mean, they had their big war, but they didn't have another like it for thousands of years. So they've learned the secret of peace, right? Not saying we put elves and gnomes in charge of Congress, but when you live that long, you've got to have more of a clue, don't you?"

"They've got a lot of people messing around doing low-level shitty stuff, including elves and gnomes." James narrowed his eyes. "I've met far too many Oriceran pieces of shit to believe they're any better than humans just because they live longer. From what I've read, and Shay's told me, the war lasted generations. It'd be something we could barely imagine, and this stupid soldier factory is barely functioning at a way lower capacity than it could be in a magic-rich environment. Who knows what happens, say, five hundred years from now, when something like this gets set off? Does Texas cease to exist?"

Harper rolled her eyes. "You know they say you get out of the world what you put into it, and you're putting in really dreary vibes, pseudo-Dad. Try to look on the bright side. Magic: cool. New opportunities. New ways of healing people."

"And new ways of killing people. Lots of new ways. I have spent most of my adult life dealing with those new ways."

Harper blew a raspberry. "That's like saying technology is bad because they invented guns, bombs, and nukes."

"If you hadn't convinced me to come here, you might not have been able to find anyone," James suggested. "And this thing might already be overwhelming a nearby town. This shit is dangerous, and this kind of magic is dangerous. The people who made this shit are dangerous. Now, I don't think they're any more dangerous than humans, but there are no enlightened races coming to lead us to a golden age. There are just some nice people who live longer and some assholes who live longer."

"Your wife must be a saint to put up with you," Harper murmured.

Light thuds echoed down the hallway from above. Shadows danced on the wall ahead from one of the tunnels connected to another six-way intersection.

"Get behind me," James ordered.

Harper wagged a finger but complied. "See, now the universe is punishing us for your pessimism."

A dense pack of soldiers rushed around the corner. They stopped and raised their hands, opening their palms up flat. The light slowly grew in intensity.

"What the hell are they doing?" James asked. "Why aren't they attacking? Recon?"

Harper backed away. "I don't know. Maybe you should go over and ask them."

Bright orange energy blasts shot from their palms. The volley struck James, exploding against and knocking him to the ground, blowing several smoking craters in his armor. Soil fell from the walls and ceiling, leaving a shallow layer over him. Harper yelped and ducked.

Adaptation in progress, Whispy declared. *Regeneration in progress.* The symbiont's euphoria washed away some of James' irritation.

He grunted and got to one knee. "Huh. Nice hit, I'll give them that."

"Ouch." Harper grimaced. "You okay?"

"I'm fine." James stood, pain spreading over his chest.

Another volley followed. James grunted. The second attack stung but didn't knock him over. The pain began to fade.

High adaptation achieved, his symbiont reported. *Regeneration remains in progress.*

James snarled and sprinted toward the soldiers. They

spent less time charging up their attacks, instead pelting him with quick shots that stopped stinging after a couple of seconds. He arrived at their line and impaled two with one blow. Their clouds of smoke obscured the others as some clawed at James and others continued firing. The holes in his armor started to fill as he slashed and stabbed his way through the mob of enemies.

An explosion shook the cavern and he spun around. Harper lay on the ground, grimacing, blood running down the side of her face, and there was a pink glow around her body for a few seconds before it faded. Rock and dirt sealed one of the tunnels.

A surge from the soldiers forced James' attention back to the enemies. He extended another blade as he rushed back into the smoke, swinging, slicing and stabbing, his growls and grunts some of the few sounds other than the pop of the enemies' energy blasts and the scrapes of their claws against his armor. The furious melee in the narrow space finished with him slicing a magical soldier into four pieces, but the choking smoke made it hard to see anything.

Harper approached, her slender shadow readily distinguishable from the bulkier enemy forms. "Sorry about the distraction, but I had to blow the tunnel. There were like forty of them coming from the other side."

"Did you just bury us in here?" James growled.

"Of course not." Harper shrugged. "At least, I think not. We came a different way. And even if I did, I'm sure you could dig us out. I've seen stuff on the net. I know you can fire a big magic beam." She coughed on the smoke and waved her hand. Much of it had settled near the ground in a thick obscuring layer. "But we better find the core quickly. You might not care if a hundred of those guys show up at once, but I don't know how long my shields will hold." She held up the soot-covered crystal. "I'm pretty sure we're close anyway." She jogged forward and motioned for him to follow. "Come on, pseudo-Dad. I'll make you proud."

James went after her. His regeneration had eliminated the pain and repaired most of his armor, but the fact that the soldiers had hurt him twice didn't escape him. Either they had been holding back previously, or they really *were* adapting. It made sense. There was no reason to believe the Vax symbionts possessed an ability unique in the universe.

A few minutes of jogging brought James and Harper to another intersection.

"Damn it," she muttered. "I thought we'd get there by now." She groaned and pointed. "Oh, come on, already. This is getting obnoxious."

James turned as a horde of soldiers rushed down a connected tunnel. The dim lighting made it difficult to count, but there must have been at least twice as many as the last batch. They raised their palms and fired a massive volley. The shots barely stung this time.

Near maximum adaptation achieved, Whispy reported.

"Don't get killed," he ordered Harper. "And seal every tunnel but the direction we came from, the one I'm about to go into and the direction we need to go. I'll go finish them."

Whispy, after we finish them off, I'm gonna feed you again, and we're going extended advanced.

Kill the enemy, Whispy replied.

That's the plan.

A few minutes later, James made his way down the smoky tunnel, claws on his hands and his helmet surrounding his head. Harper stood in the center of the previous intersection, now even paler than before, having collapsed three of the tunnels.

Harper patted her backpack. "Just so you know, I've only got two more of those particular explosive beans."

"Explosive beans? Seriously?"

"You use what's useful in my line of work, whether it's cool or not." Harper shrugged, then pointed at his helmet. "They getting tougher?"

"Not so much, but it doesn't hurt to be prepared." James indicated another tunnel. "This way?"

"Yeah." Harper held out the crystal to verify and nodded before heading forward. "You're just like them, aren't you?"

James walked slightly in front of her, his expanded range of vision making it easy for him to not get too far ahead of his temporary partner. "Like who?"

"The soldiers the Seasons of Rage create," Harper explained, gesturing at his armor. "You adapt to things."

He didn't respond. It wasn't like no one knew that fact, but it wasn't something most of the international or LA underworld understood. A lot of them just assumed he was ridiculously tough, which was why assholes like Jolly Jonathan sometimes thought they had a chance, with sufficient preparation.

"You don't have to admit it," she continued. "I can tell."

She twirled, a delighted look on her face. "I told you. I'm smart, and I'm good at noticing things. It's one of the reasons I've been able to gather the collection of artifacts I have. I've never been the toughest, most ruthless, or strongest woman, but I have a fine and keen eye for details others miss. It's not like me knowing that will help me. Even if I wanted to sell the information, you've spent years as a bounty hunter. You've probably adapted to almost anything anyone can think of."

James grunted. "Let's drop the sub—" A half-dozen soldiers rushed down their original tunnel toward Harper's back. He spun and charged the woman.

She threw up her hands. "Pseudo-Dad, we can work this..." Her voice trailed off as James rushed past her in time to take the blasts from the soldiers.

He raised his arm and charged a cannon blast, then carved through the enemy with a sustained green energy beam.

"Woah," Harper declared. "That could have hurt."

James growled. "We're running out of time. Let's go."

Harper swallowed and sped up. They passed through two additional intersections before their next tunnel widened. The air shimmered and crackled at the mouth of the tunnel, which led to a vast spherical chamber. Six small glowing stone pyramids of different colors from red to indigo hovered in the center of the chamber. It was otherwise featureless, except for the small dais on the opposite end.

"That's the core," Harper announced, pointing at the dais. "It was on the surface when I left. I just need to jam this crystal in there and sing the sequence."

"'Sing the sequence?'" James looked at her like she'd lost her mind. She'd sung earlier, but he'd thought she was just quirky.

"I didn't build it." Harper shrugged, looking more amused than worried.

"If that's the core, where do they make the soldiers?" James asked.

"In the little soldier nursery?" She shrugged and laughed. "I don't know. Before, they just appeared behind me. Besides, in a couple of minutes, it won't matter anymore." She reached into her backpack and pulled out a small clay tablet with crude pictographs. "This little non-paying gig is using up most of my best gear, but we need to get past that shield first, so here it goes." She hurled the tablet at the mouth of the tunnel.

The tablet exploded into thousands of slivers and the entire tunnel shook. The shimmers and crackling stopped.

James rushed forward, looking around for enemies but seeing nothing. "This should be easy. I'll just guard the door while you do your pop-star impression."

A ray of energy shot from each pyramid toward the dais. Each ray terminated on the ground about a yard apart. New soldiers shimmered into existence in different locations. While they were similar in appearance to James' previous foes, each was the color of its source pyramid and twice the height of a standard soldier.

High potential for additional adaptation, Whispy suggested.

"Well, that's not very fair," Harper muttered.

"Watch the back tunnel," James ordered. "Seal it if you need to. You're right. If necessary, I'll try to dig us out of here, but we might get flanked while I fight the officers here, or whatever you want to call them."

Harper folded her arms and tapped her foot, wearing an impatient look on her face. "Hurry up, pseudo-Dad. This is beginning to get a little annoying."

CHAPTER SEVENTEEN

O *kay, what do we got? Red, orange, yellow, green, blue,*
and purple, huh? Almost all the colors of the rainbow. It's
time for them to taste some pain.

James stomped forward, sweeping his blades back and
forth to aim at his different enemies. The officers all slowly
spread apart, forming a growing half-moon. They lifted
their arms, their palms glowing brighter with each move-
ment, but like their smaller cousins, they didn't talk or
make any sort of vocalization.

"Come on, assholes," he shouted. "Let's see if you got
anything new. Big, impressive Oriceran death factory. You
can't handle one James Brownstone. Does this mean I
would have won the Great War by myself?"

All six officers fired at once, producing a loud,
resounding pop. The blow struck James, and the resulting
massive explosion enveloped him. He hissed in pain as he
flew through the air. His flight ended in a collision with a
wall, and he fell to the ground with holes pitting his armor
all over and deep burns covering his exposed flesh.

Fuckers. Can't take a little trash talk?

Yessssss, Whispy cheered. *New adaptations in progress. Regeneration in progress.*

James growled and hopped back to his feet, his entire body now an open nerve. "Congratulations, assholes. This is the best workout I've gotten in almost ten years, but the rule is, you take me down on the first hit or you don't take me down at all. Now it's my turn to repay the favor."

The officers fired again. James grunted and jerked back as shots exploded around him again. This time, the attack didn't sear off any armor, but it did sting, and aggravated his existing injuries.

High adaptation achieved, Whispy reported. *Rerouting some resources to regeneration.*

The pain lessened but didn't vanish. James crouched and leapt into the air, barely avoiding another volley that blew a massive chunk out of the wall and elicited a yelp from Harper in the tunnel. His arc took him toward the yellow officer, and as he fell, he pointed his blades at the chest of the magically conjured opponent.

James snarled as his blades struck the yellow warrior and bounced off with a clang. The enemies quickly surrounded him and began rapid-firing at point-blank range. The attacks stung, but proved more distracting than deadly. He swung a blade at the green officer, and while it managed to cut the outer layer of his enemy, it still didn't penetrate into the chest.

Offensive adaptation in progress, Whispy reported. *Recommend additional attacks for adjustment. Other adaptations in progress. Regeneration in progress.*

Several of the officers clawed at him, but their attacks

scraped across the surface of his armor, making unpleasant noises but not doing much damage. James spun and delivered a solid kick to the purple officer, sending him flying before charging right into the green officer and bowling him over.

The opening allowed him to escape the firing cage. Much of his pain had dulled, and thin layers of armor now covered all previously exposed wounds. Tendrils continued to flow into the other holes to fill in the damage.

They don't know who they're fucking with. That should be on my tombstone if I ever die. Here lies James Brownstone. Nobody knew who they were fucking with.

Engage and kill the enemy, Whispy demanded. *High levels of adaptation achieved in current battle situation.*

If a giddy cheer had a mental texture, the symbiont's current projected feelings were close.

The officers all backed away, not launching any new attacks and staying close to the dais. There went James' secondary plan of drawing them away while Harper shut the system down.

He roared in frustration. They might not be hurting him much, but his attacks weren't accomplishing a lot either. It'd been a long time since that was a problem.

If I fed you everything I've got, can we go Forerunner?

Very low probability of success. Require substantial external power supplementation, Whispy reported.

Fine. We'll fuck these bastards up just with extended advanced.

James threw up his blades and begin charging a twin beam attack. He wasn't ready to lose. It was just a matter of attacking until he adapted to the enemy. The Vax weren't feared through the galaxy because they lost. They were the kind of beings you blew up entire cities, if not planets, to stop. He couldn't lose to some Oriceran war factory.

The purple officer turned in Harper's direction and raised his arms, powering up his own attack. James released his beams, and the combined blast punched through the enemy's chest and launched the magical creation backward. It started turning into dust before it hit the ground.

James roared in approval over the kill before charging up another attack. The officers all opened fire again, a near-constant stream of attacks pelting his halfway-repaired armor. He ignored the stings from the underlying partially healed wounds. Bright green sparks intensified across his blades. A moment later, another blast ripped from James and cut through the red officer.

He barked mocking laughter. "I told you you had one shot, assholes. I hope somewhere in those little magical brains, you all understand you're about to die. I didn't even want to be here, and I'm taking it out on all of you."

James' third blast erupted and struck the chest of the orange officer, but the beams bounced off at an angle like sunlight hitting a mirror and struck the ceiling. Rock and dirt showered down from above.

Huh. Okay, that's not gonna work, so we're doing this a different way.

He retracted one of the blades and sprinted toward the orange officer. The enemies continued their desperate firing. He stabbed and slashed, growling and snarling at the enemy construct, the blade sinking deeper with each attack.

Individual offensive adaptation achieved, Whispy reported after his seventh thrust.

James roared and plunged the blade into the energy heart of the officer. The large foe jerked and slumped to the ground, turning into smoke. The survivors, yellow, green, and blue, backed away from James toward the dais. They ceased fire.

"Afraid?" He snorted. "You should be. I'm James Brownstone. The Granite Ghost. The Scourge of Harriken. I've fought everything from necromancers to nightmares haunting entire races, and I'm not gonna lose to the likes of you weak-ass fuckers."

Bright blinding light erupted from all three officers. James' helmet filters allowed him to stare directly at them as the three officers walked into each other, their intensity increasing. The bodies melted together, twisting and flowing into each other over several seconds until the light vanished.

They were gone, replaced by a six-legged, six-armed creature with three heads. Their different colors had been replaced by a dull ochre glow around the new monster's face and arms. Glowing whip-like extensions grew from the arms.

James glanced at the tunnel. Harper was gone. He wasn't sure if he was disappointed or surprised she had lasted as long as she had.

Finally ran, huh? Whatever. I'm sure I can just blow this thing to hell once I'm done with Mr. Triple Threat here.

The entire chamber shook violently for several seconds. The pyramids all dimmed; recharging, maybe. It didn't matter. He figured without the Eye of Winter, he would just incinerate the core and the artifacts.

The new monstrosity galloped toward James and pelted him with its whips. The first few blows cut deep, slicing through his armor like it wasn't even there. He leapt out of reach, his teeth gritted, doing his best to ignore the pain.

These fuckers really can *adapt.*

Adaptation in progress, Whispy reported. *Regeneration in progress.* Waves of satisfaction and happiness radiated from the symbiont. *Continue to engage and kill enemy.*

His enemy charged again, striking furiously with the whips. The blows stung, but this time, they didn't strip off or cut through his armor. James sliced through two of them and the whips fell to the floor, writhing for a few seconds before adding to the low-lying smoke layer.

High adaptation achieved, Whispy sent. *Near maximum adaptation for attack-type approaching.*

This might be fun for you, but I've had enough.

James stomped toward his opponent, his irritation building. He let out a long, low growl. "I was supposed to just be working at the restaurant and waiting for my new kid, you combo asshole."

The monster swung its remaining whips. James caught one with a clawed hand and sliced it off with his blade. The other two blows bounced off his nearly-regenerated armor.

James snorted. "The only thing that was supposed to be challenged was my palate," he bellowed. "By that fucking pineapple magic-cow steak! What the fuck was up with that, Nadina?" He jumped toward his opponent and severed the remaining whips. Two legs kicked at him, but he threw up his arm, absorbing the blow with ease. "Then some arrogant-ass tuxedo-wearing wizard decided he needed to fuck with me, and that meant I had to go to this fucking annoying pizza place and sign autographs." He rushed forward and cut a leg off. "And then I had to go on a road trip with a vegan. A *vegan!*" He cut another leg off.

His enemy turned and clawed at him, but the blows bounced off his armor. There was almost no pain this time, and the discomfort from before had faded.

"And finally I had to go into this fucking maze-hole with all you assholes, who don't even have the decency to be scared when I fuck you up, which means I have to waste time killing you over and over and over." James removed the remaining legs with quick, precise cuts. He followed up by slicing off the arms. "And all of this required me to follow a manic-sociopathic pixie-girl around when I should be at home with my fucking wife, who is about to give birth!" He extended a second blade, then shoved his weapons into the center of the combined body and swung out with both hands, slicing what remained of the combined body in half.

The pieces collapsed to the ground, slowly vaporizing into the acrid smoke clinging to half the chamber.

"I am not a fucking superhero!" James roared. "I'm barely a bounty hunter anymore. I'm a damned pitmaster!" He growled and looked around for something else to kill. When no new soldiers, officers, or monsters appeared, he retracted his helmet and snorted. "And now I have to figure out how to shut this shit down by myself because Harper dragged my ass here and ran."

A shadow with no source moved on a nearby wall. He spun toward it, his eyes narrowed. "Buy a clue."

Harper winked into existence and waved. "Easy-peasy, right? Sorry. I just got a little freaked by the whole giant monster trying to kill me earlier thing, but that was a, like, grade-A ass-kicking. I would pay to see that kind of thing. Not lying." She yanked the crystal chain off her neck. "And now it's time to shut this bad boy down." She sashayed over toward the dais, humming a jaunty tune that vaguely reminded him of the one he had heard at Amazing Dwayne's. While it was obviously a different song when he thought about it, the reminder of his previous annoyance flooded into his mind. A sudden thought invaded it and colonized the space.

"Wait," James shouted. "Something doesn't make sense," he explained. "You're just going to shut it off?"

"Sure." Harper shook the crystal. "Remember, I've got the Eye of Winter, and I know the song sequence." She sang the last few words and danced a little.

"Why does this thing even still exist?" James gestured around the chamber.

"Huh? Is this like, 'If a gnome farts in the woods and no one is there to hear him, does he make a sound?'"

"Something just doesn't feel right. It hasn't for a while."

Harper stared at him, her smile slowly fading. "You didn't just come here because your wife told you to, did you?"

James shrugged. "This shit is dangerous. If I let it spread, I'd have to deal with it eventually. I'm taking care of the annoyance now."

"Because it might hurt a bunch of random people?"

Harper replied, her face twisted in a grimace. "Come on. The US has nukes, and the PDA has all sorts of stuff. They could call the Oricerans and reach out to that Fixer guy. It's not like they couldn't have stopped this thing, but you came here and risked your life for people you don't even know." She jabbed at the air with her finger. "And this thing kept adapting to you. It could have killed you. Don't tell me it couldn't have. I saw it mess you up a bunch of times."

"It takes a lot to kill me. You'd be surprised. I was never worried. I was mostly just pissed."

"Why?" Harper threw up her hands. "Why do you even *care*? Do you know, when I showed up at your house, I *expected* you to say no. You were supposed to say no so I'd have an excuse to run!" She ruffled her hair with both hands. "And then you said yes, and I didn't have an excuse, so here I am, also risking my life in this hole."

"I'm not gonna apologize for helping clean up your mistake," James rumbled.

Harper rolled her eyes so hard it looked like she was having a seizure. "Do you think any of the people in the towns and cities you just helped save care? They will go about their days, probably not caring about you at all, if they even think about you. If they do hear about you, it's just because you're this famous guy they find cool. It's not like they give a shit. No one does, and you're risking your life for *them*? Why?"

James stared at her. She looked away.

"You're risking your life for them too," he observed. "You didn't have to. You could have run. You didn't have to come find me."

"It was my mistake," Harper replied softly, tears welling in the corners of her eyes. "I'm not going to say it's my responsibility. It's ultimately the fault of the Oriceran assholes who made this thing and the Southguards, but..." She shook her fists. "It was never supposed to be in the middle of Texas. Damn it. I'm sure even the stupid Southguards aren't evil enough to drop it just anywhere. They probably would keep it in a vault because they knew if they ever used it, the PDA would teleport in a nuke or something." She sighed and lowered her head. "We don't have a lot of time. You need to get going right now." She lifted her head. "Before it's too late. It's my mistake, and I'll handle it."

CHAPTER EIGHTEEN

James frowned. "I'm gonna be honest with you. I'm kind of pissed, tired, and all sorts of annoyed. I get that you're trying to fuck me over, but I don't get how. I'm a simple man. I love my wife, my kids, and barbeque. Break it down for me, Rabbit Girl. I'm trying to figure out if I should be grateful or if I should cut you in half. Right now, both seem reasonable.

Recommend bisection, Whispy suggested.

You always recommend whatever kills people, James thought back. *Shut up for now. I'm having trouble concentrating.*

Harper let out a long sigh. "The disarming system does take down everything, including all the soldiers. That's all true. But I did leave a few details out. The Eye of Winter isn't just a key. It activates a total self-destruct."

"So? That's a good thing. The world will be better off without this Seasons of Rage shit. No one needs a magical automated death factory."

"Here's the trick, though. It's not just the Eye of Winter

you need to fully activate the self-destruct system." Harper glanced at the dais. "They wanted this thing to be *really* hard to take down unless you were damned sure. The person with the Eye has to stick around for a certain period or it cancels the self-destruct. There's a lag, you see. I don't know how long it is, but everything I know says that it's long enough that the created complex is going to collapse with the person still inside." Her shoulders slumped. "I didn't care before because I had a way to portal out, but I had to use it to get to LA, so I came up with a solution." She pointed at James. "I needed a patsy, but I also needed someone to help me fight my way in. There is no song of activation. You just need someone to jam the stupid Eye of Winter in a slot on the dais. I lied about that so you wouldn't have a reason to call the PDA and just hand it over to them, and then I figured I could convince you to stay here while it armed the system and I ran my ass to the surface and escaped. No prison, everyone's saved, and I'm not dead."

James furrowed his brow, confusion nibbling at the budding anger. "You think I'm that easy to manipulate?"

"Yes. I know what you see when you look at me. A wayward little lamb who needs the guidance of pseudo-Dad Brownstone, just like Alison did." Harper kicked a pebble. "I'm not like your daughter, James. I told you before that I'm not a good person who missed out on childhood opportunities. I'm a selfish bitch who has to risk her life constantly just to feel like I'm alive. You're right. I have no idea how many people I've hurt over the years since I figured if I wasn't pulling the trigger, it wasn't my fault. It was the only way I could sleep at night."

Kill the enemy, Whispy suggested.

Sometimes the enemy's hard to determine, James responded.

No. Kill the enemy.

James gestured at the dais. "Why are you telling me now? Is this another con? I'm not gonna stick around so you can run just because you told me the truth if that's what you're thinking. This isn't one of those I-respect-your-bravery things. I have a wife, a kid, and another kid coming. I have too much to live for."

Harper shook her head, her peppy mask abandoned, replaced by glum reality. "Because I couldn't do it. You sicken me." She sneered. "And everything I've seen you do on our little road trip together has sickened me even more."

"Why is that?" James was more curious than annoyed, but it was hard to concentrate with Whispy insisting on her death every few seconds.

"Because you make me feel bad about myself," Harper shouted. She slapped her chest. "I'm supposed to be looking out for Number One."

"And how am I stopping you?"

Harper threw her back and let out a hysterical laugh. "Do you understand what we're in? It's a death factory. Even with my dampening it, and it just starting to power up, it would have killed a lot of normal people, even on Oriceran. It adapts to its foes, but you were cutting through and blasting them to bits like they were made of paper. If they sent the Army in here in power armor, they would have taken heavy casualties, but here you are, unscathed."

James shrugged. "If I'd died on the way, your plan wouldn't have worked anyway."

"Don't you get it? You're one of the toughest people on Earth, and now that I understand more about how your armor works, I'm even more convinced of that. And what do you do with all that power? You run a barbeque restaurant!" Harper groaned. "Who does that? That's crazy! *You're* crazy."

"I like barbeque," he complained. "I know you don't get that with your alien vegan mind, but a lot of people like barbeque. It's tasty, and it makes people feel good. Not like your rabbit food."

"Forget the damned barbeque, James!" Harper shouted. "The point is, you could go somewhere and use your power. You could take over a country on Earth, or even a country on Oriceran. You defeated the queen of the Drow. You could become King of Brownstonia, and you haven't. You're cooking barbeque. Don't you see why that's infuriating?"

Whispy had gone quiet, which allowed James to concentrate. Not that it helped.

"No," James replied. "I don't get why that's pissing you off so much. Why do you care if I don't go around being a prick? It doesn't affect you either way."

Harper closed her eyes and took a deep breath. "It's not like I've studied your life or anything, but you *are* pretty famous. I just kept thinking that as we spent time together, I'd see that you were just like me. That you were nothing more than a mercenary who got off on excitement and risking his life. Or even that you just really liked hurting people because you're a sadist. But you're not. I get it now.

You want people to think that, but it's not what you are, and it makes me question everything."

She held up the crystal. "Coming here. I said it was about limits, but it wasn't. Not really. It was about saving my ass. If I let this thing get out of control, by the time the government got done cleaning it up, they'd investigate, and that investigation would lead to me someday, and I wouldn't end up in prison. They'd execute me. It was always more about saving my butt than anything else." She glared at him. "Why couldn't you have been a mercenary bastard? It would have made it easier."

He shrugged. "Sorry. It's hard to be a complete bastard when you're married to someone like Shay and have a daughter like Alison. If I become too much of a fucker, they'd smack me around until I came back to my senses. Not to mention Father McCartney, Mack, and Trey...and Maria. And Tyler would get all smug. The last thing I want to do is give him a reason to be smug." He grunted. "It's less annoying to not be a complete asshole. I'm all about keeping my life as simple as possible."

James considered some of what he had just said. It was true Shay and Alison gave him a fundamental reason to get up each day, but Father Thomas' sacrifice so long ago had etched itself on his soul. At some level, he wondered if he'd also always felt in his heart that the deaths of his parents had saved him from being another mindless Vax sacrifice.

"Damn you, James Brownstone." Harper wiped away tears. "Get out of here." She marched toward the dais. "For once in my self-absorbed life, I'll do something for someone other than me." She stopped in front of the dais. "You might be tough, James, but if you get buried by tons of rock and soil, even you might end up dead, or sitting in the ground for fifty years going nuts or something. Everyone says you have a pretty good memory. You can find your way back, right?"

He nodded slowly. "Yeah, that's not a problem."

"Would a ten-minute head start be enough?" Harper asked.

"Since I've still got my armor on, if I sprinted, yeah, that would do it."

Harper nodded at the tunnel. "Then get going. The longer you wait, the more chance reinforcements will show up. Beating down those six guardians seems to have reset the system somehow, but the light on the artifacts has been getting steadily brighter. So go."

Sorry, Shay. I'm about to do something you probably won't like.

"If you had your portal artifact from before, you could have escaped?" James asked. "You couldn't have spared a day to go hit up a black-market contact for a new one?"

"Because I had *so* much time to consider the situation." Harper rolled her eyes like she was dealing with a frustrating younger brother. "You know one of the reasons I don't use a lot of portal artifacts? It's because I have all my dampening and nullification artifacts. Rings, my sweater, some papers in my pockets, and a few other things. The one I used before was calibrated in a particular way, so my other artifacts didn't interfere with it. Even if I found another portal artifact, I would have to leave behind all my gear to escape with it, and there was no way I was going into an Oriceran death factory without my dampeners.

Who cares? I don't have one now anyway. So go, before I change my mind."

James reached toward his leg. The armor opened and a tendril extended, portal stone in hand, taken from his pocket. "One-way portal stone."

Harper's eyes widened. "Seriously?"

"You're gonna have to leave behind all the crap you talked about, but at least you'll be alive. I figure that's a good trade-off. Just ask yourself how much your life is worth."

"Why?" Harper asked, her voice barely a whisper.

James grinned. "Because when the choice finally came, you chose to be a human being and not a selfish little shit."

Harper laughed. "Thanks, pseudo-Dad." She sniffled and dropped her backpack on the ground before stripping off most of her rings. She then yanked several yellowed pieces of paper out of pockets, tossed them to the ground, and finished by pulling off her sweater. "I really liked that sweater, too. It was part of my signature look."

"Buy a new one." James walked toward the dais. "Once I open the portal, it'll only hold for ten seconds. This might take careful timing."

"You're sure?" Harper asked. "I wouldn't save my ass if I were you."

"I've known a lot of people who have turned their lives around. You've still got your money, right? You can go hide on your island for a while until the Southguards forget about all of it. Or fake your own death. I know people with experience in that kind of thing."

"I bet you do." Harper managed a playful grin as she

lowered the crystal toward a slot in the dais. "Congratulations, pseudo-Dad. We defeated an Oriceran death factory as part of our road-trip bonding experience." She winked, her cheek still pinks from her tears, and shoved the crystal into the dais.

The entire cavern shook.

"How long do you have to stay?" James asked, regretting not having asked that question earlier.

Recommend immediate evacuation, Whispy sent.

Just wait a second.

"The dais will turn to smoke," Harper shouted over the roar of the quake. She licked her lips, her eyes darting around. "That's when I'll know the sequence is irreversible."

The tremors intensified, and portions of the chamber roof fell, leaving large piles of dirt and rock on the floor.

"Come on, come on, come on," she muttered. "Just disappear."

James raised the portal stone. He opened his mouth and prepared to swallow.

Extreme danger, Whispy reported. *Again recommend immediate evacuation.*

Jagged cracks of light shot through the pyramids in the center of the room. The artifacts collapsed and shattered into multiple pieces with loud booms.

Harper closed her eyes. "I guess this is what they call karma."

The bottom of the dais darkened and drifted upward as smoke. A few seconds later, the rest of it finished the transformation. James plopped the stone into this mouth and swallowed, concentrating on the Toyota outside. A few seconds later, a portal with a bright, juddering edge opened in front of him. He grabbed Harper, who still had her eyes closed, and leapt through.

They appeared beside the parked vehicle. Even at this distance from the tunnels, the violent shaking of the ground almost knocked them off their feet. A few seconds later, six columns of colored light blasted through the ground and shot into the sky, leaving behind a twinkling trail as they faded over the next ten seconds.

"Woah." Harper tapped one of her few remaining rings and summoned a new light orb. She threw her arms around James and gave him a tight hug. "We did it, and you saved me. Thanks, pseudo-Dad."

James extricated himself from the woman. "You really need to stop calling me that. It's annoying as shit."

She frowned. "Why did you portal us back here instead of LA?"

"I figure you're gonna need to go to Austin to get a new start on your life. I'm gonna drive back and grab some barbeque at a bunch of places we missed." James shrugged. "And not bringing you back to LA decreases the chance my wife will slit your throat once she finds out you planned to betray me."

"You don't think she'll forgive me for telling the truth?" Harper sounded hopeful.

"I think you don't fuck with anyone important to Shay and live long," James explained.

"She's not just a college professor, is she?" Harper's grin consumed her face.

"Everyone has a past. Some people just bury theirs better than others."

Harper laced her fingers together and stretched her

arms above her head. "I just left behind millions of dollars' worth of artifacts because I decided to save a bunch of random Texans. How messed up is that? I'm a vegan. I'm like the natural enemy of Texans."

James turned toward the car. "Then we should get—"

Bright portals opened, and four men in dark clothing stepped out, wands in hand and light orbs hovering over them. Twenty other men rushed out of the portals, all holding rifles, shimmering layers of light covering their bodies. Shield spells.

New enemies identified, Whispy reported. *Engage and kill.*

A helmet slid closed around James' head. It was just one of those nights.

CHAPTER NINETEEN

E ven though James had a good idea as to the answer, he still needed to ask the obvious question. He had no problem killing people, but he liked to know who he was killing.

"Who the fuck are you?" he bellowed.

One of the wizards smiled; his bearing suggested he was the leader of the group. "We're private collection agents." He lifted his wand and murmured a spell. A huge light orb appeared and illuminated the entire area. "Right now, we represent the Southguard family."

"They're a bunch of worthless shits."

The wizard smiled but it didn't reach his eyes. "Sure, but that's not really my problem, is it? They rather generously paid a certain courier to deliver an item, and said courier disappeared with the item. We need to collect the item and deliver it to our employers, along with the courier. She's been real hard to track until just now. I guess it's our lucky night."

"The item? You mean the Seasons of Rage?"

The wizard sighed. "I need the six pyramids. I assume since you two are here that they're around here somewhere. Where are they?"

I'm so not in the mood for this shit.

Kill the enemy, Whispy suggested.

You'd say that if I was in the mood for this shit too.

Always a sound tactical suggestion.

James looked at the surrounding men. "The Southguards don't need a portable war factory. This planet doesn't. It'd be annoying as fuck for a lot of people with better things to do with their time." He nodded in the direction of the former tunnel complex. "And it doesn't matter since it's gone anyway."

The wizard frowned. "Gone? Where is it? Who has it?" Desperation and irritation mixed in his voice.

"No one has it," James explained. "It blew up. The core and the pyramids are all gone." He pantomimed an explosion. "Turns out the thing has a self-destruct system. We set it off, and so now the Seasons of Rage have gone onto messed-up artifact heaven. Your employers will need to time-travel if they want a new one."

"Why should I believe you?" the wizard demanded.

James shrugged. "Don't believe me. I don't give a shit. It's the truth. You said yourself you were having trouble tracking Harper, and suddenly you could. Think about why that might be."

The wizard's jaw clenched. "That's very unfortunate since it means, among other things, we're not going to get a bonus from our employers, but we still can complete our secondary task." He smiled at Harper. "That woman's coming with us. She owes an explanation to our mutual employers."

Harper waggled her fingers with a mocking smile on her face. "There's no way I'm going with you guys. That would be the stupidest thing I could do, and I've done a lot of stupid things tonight." She gestured at James with both hands. "And I'm with him right now. After what I've just seen him do, it's hard to be afraid of you guys. It'd be hard to be afraid of twice as many guys. You honestly think you can win against *the* James Brownstone?"

The wizard kept his wand up as he looked at James and Harper. "Yeah, it's not like anyone else uses that kind of armor. I thought it was you, but I was hoping it wasn't."

James retracted his helmet for a few seconds before closing it again. "That help?"

"Shit," one of the men with rifles murmured. "It is him."

The wizard nodded. "That changes nothing. You're no bodyguard, and we've got no beef with you, Brownstone, but we need that woman. So you took down the Seasons. Not my problem. That's the Southguards' problem. But she needs to come with us."

"So the Southguards can kill her?" James asked. "That's how this ends. Tell me I'm wrong."

"Did she give you some sob story?" The wizard sneered. "Trust me. If you think my employers are such pieces of shit, you need to ask yourself why she was working for them to begin with. She'd slit your throat if she thought she could make a profit off it."

That's what this is, James thought. *She's like a younger Shay and a younger Alison. Fuck it. I've got nothing better to do.*

James extended a blade. The men all stepped back and pointed their weapons and wands at him.

"Give me one good reason I should turn her over to you assholes," he growled. "And don't tell me it's so you can make money. I don't give two fucks whether or not you make money. Let's get that clear right here and now."

"She's not a good person, Brownstone," the wizard insisted. "Isn't that a good enough reason? She's garbage. Trash."

"That's okay. I'm not a good person either, but like you said, I've got no beef with you."

The wizard nodded, giving him a hungry grin. "Exactly. I don't know how you got roped into this, and honestly, given what that thing is, it's probably best that you took it down, but it's time to punish the woman responsible."

Harper sighed and stepped forward, defeat written on her face.

"The people responsible are dust on Oriceran." James put up his arm to block Harper. "You're all fancy with your portals. That makes this easy. I'll give you thirty seconds to portal on out of here before I get more irritated than I already am."

"Are you shitting me?" The wizard glared at him. "You're making a mistake. Every man here who isn't using a wand has anti-magic bullets. We don't want to fight you, but it's not like we *can't*. You don't want to make an enemy like the Southguards."

"I think you've got this backward," he replied.

"Oh?" The wizard smirked. "How do you figure?"

James raised his blade. "They don't want to make an enemy like *me*."

"Fuck this." The wizard shouted an incantation. A fire-ball streaked from his wand toward James. It exploded against his chest, the sensation barely noticeable.

Maximum adaptation already achieved against attack type, Whispy reported. *Kill and terminate all enemies rapidly to minimize inefficiency.*

Harper dropped behind the car, covering her head. The other three wizards fired blue-white stun bolts. The attacks slammed into James, the energy arcing along the armor for a few seconds before dissipating.

"That was a big mistake." He took a single step forward.

The wizard leader gritted his teeth. "Fire, you idiots. Weaken his defenses so we can finish him off already."

A hail of bullets filled the air. The expensive rounds bounced off James, not even stinging. Several bullets struck the car, ripping through the body or the windows. Two of the tires popped, and the car sank on one side. James continued walking forward at a slow, methodical pace, a constant plink of rounds colliding with him.

They must be getting a shitload of money to not have run once they realized it was me.

The wizard leader pointed his wand at the car, muttering quickly under his breath. The vehicle rose into the air and floated over James. Harper scurried along the ground, low-crawling through the shrubs as bullets flew over her, her cover gone.

James whipped up his blade as the Toyota dropped. He sliced through the vehicle, sparks flying, before the two halves fell on either side of him with a loud crunch.

The gunmen continued to pepper him with bullets. The other wizards cycled through different attacks. An ice lance cracked as it smashed into his side. A glob of acid sizzled as it dripped off his arm and ate away at the forest floor. A pulsating and spiraling orange lance erupted from one wand and exploded in a shower of sparks against his shoulder, leaving a slight scorch mark and stinging but not accomplishing anything else. One dark beam tickled.

Whispy repeated the same report. *Maximum adaptation already achieved against attack types.*

"He's got to be reaching his limit," the wizard leader shouted. "Keep going. We can win this. He can't even attack."

James grinned underneath his helmet. Harper had been right. There were few regular enemies on Earth who had a chance of breaching his defenses in extended advanced mode after years of adaptation, including purposeful and directed training of the symbiont. It'd taken an ancient Oriceran war machine to hurt him a little, and now the Seasons of Rage were destroyed—just like his current opponents would soon be if they didn't surrender. He stopped walking forward.

"See?" the wizard leader commented. "I told he was reaching his limit."

He jerked his wand to the side, not to attack Harper, but to slice a tree through the base and drop it on top of James. The modest trunk bounced off his armor with a dull thud, the wood cracking. The gunmen stopped firing and took the chance to reload. They had just ejected their magazines when a tiny stone flew past James.

Wait. Is that a bean?

The bean arced toward the back of the group, and they either ignored it or didn't see it. Disregarding the massive explosion afterward proved more difficult. Screams filled the night. Bodies, rifles, and wands flew through the air, and when the flames and smoke cleared, a massive smoldering crater marred the forest floor. Half the attack force lay on the ground, either dead or wounded. James looked behind him. Harper was crouching behind a tree with a smirk on her face.

James pointed his blade at the wizard leader, who now lay on the ground groaning, blood matting his hair to his forehead. "You haven't even scratched me, and it looks like the woman you were supposed to capture could have taken you out easily even without my help. Do you really want to continue this? Is a paycheck worth dying for? I could cut you fuckers down like nothing, but I'm tired, and I just want to get a goodnight's sleep before heading back home."

The wizard leader lifted his head and gritted his teeth. "If I don't come back with something for my employers, they'll be unhappy. No one likes the Southguards when they're unhappy."

"You keep trying to fight me, I won't be unhappy, but you'll be dead." James shrugged. "However, I've got something you can give to the Southguards that will still make them unhappy, but it'll focus that on someone other than you."

The wizard leader stood and started swaying, burns on his body. He half-closed his eyes as he cast a healing spell, running his wand over his body. He sighed in relief before asking, "What's that, Brownstone?"

"A message," James rumbled. "You tell them James Brownstone blew up their toy, and if they know what's good for them, they'll just chalk this up to a sad, expensive loss and move on. If they think they can take me on, they need to study recent criminal history more thoroughly. It's been a while since I personally took down an entire organization or family, but maybe I'm due. You think you could do that for me?"

The other man offered a shallow nod. "It was nothing personal, Brownstone. It was just business. You would have done the same if our positions had been reversed."

"Nothing personal. I just kill people who try to kill me." James growled. "Now, get the fuck out of here before I decide I only need one guy to deliver the message."

The wizard leader lifted his wand and slowly chanted a spell. A moment later, a swirling portal appeared. He gestured toward it. The survivors filed through, a few pulling wounded or dead comrades. A couple of minutes later, the leader was the last to step toward the portal.

He stopped a foot away from the magical passage and looked over his shoulder. "I always wondered if it was true, but now I get it. I guess it's a good thing you opened a restaurant, so guys like me have the occasional chance of winning a fight." He snorted and stepped through the portal. It closed.

Harper staggered toward James, her smile tight. Blood soaked her shirt, and she clutched her stomach.

"You're hit?" James asked, retracting his helmet.

"Yes," she replied weakly. "Sorry it took so long. I forgot I had a few toys I didn't abandon in the tunnels."

"I could have handled those guys," James replied. "But not complaining about you taking a few down." He frowned at her wound. "I thought you had a defensive artifact? The pink force field thing?"

"It was kind of a combo defensive-slash-dampener deal, and it went up with the Seasons when I dumped all the stuff. I lost a lot of good potential backups when I left the backpack in there because it had some stuff in it that was dampening and we didn't have time to mess around." Harper sucked in a breath, shuddering. "Just so you know, I thought about giving you a big dramatic speech about what it's like to die and fake a death scene, but that would have been a pretty bitchy thing to do after you helped scare off a bunch of guys for me." Her shaking fingers slipped into her pocket and she pulled out a small vial, then removed the stopper and downed the contents. A half-minute later, her wounds had closed. "That's better. Much better. Whew. Fun, fun. I'm surprised you didn't kill all those guys."

James retracted his blade. "I didn't kill any of them, actually. You did. I was just trying to give them an out. I would have killed them if necessary, and it's too bad—for them—that it took them so long to buy a fucking clue."

Harper wrinkled her nose in disgust at the blood covering her body and legs. "I couldn't have taken that many guys by myself. They would have shot me the second I went for anything, and besides, this works out better. I'm still going to lie low for a while, but now the Southguards think I have James Brownstone's protection, which, at a minimum, will keep them from looking for me for a while."

He grunted. "You get it, then. You've got your second chance, but that doesn't mean I'm your guardian angel."

"Understood, pseudo-Dad." Harper laughed and pointed at the pieces of car. "So much for my deposit, right? I guess we can call someone to come pick us up. At least my burner phone survived all that."

"Nah. I'll jump us to the border of Austin and then we'll call someone, but I'm gonna change and go get my coat first." James nodded. "Come on." He took one last look at the crater to make sure it wasn't burning. "We'll part ways in Austin." He marched over to the car remains, then reached through the smashed window to grab the other pair of jeans, t-shirt, and boots he had brought along. "At least they have some good barbeque there."

CHAPTER TWENTY

Harper stepped away from a rental counter at the airport, keys in hand. She had a relaxed smile on her face and a bounce in her step as if she hadn't just been involved in shutting down a dangerous magical war factory and a face-off against ruthless mercenaries. James understood now that much of her personality was a façade, but it was hard for him to believe she would be acting this way after the night they had shared.

James waited in a seat across from the rental counter. He'd already rented a truck for his return trip. The woman had borrowed James' gray coat so she didn't have to explain why her clothes were covered in blood to some random airport rental car employee in the middle of the night. He'd been in that situation far too many times, but after a while, everyone always had the same response: "Oh, I see you've been busy again, Mr. Brownstone."

Harper dropped into the seat beside him and clapped once. "So this is it. We did it. Saved the world, or at least Austin." She grinned. "I know a lot of it was my fault to begin with, but it does kind of feel good to have helped people. It feels stupid, but it also feels good. I also think we made a good team."

James grunted. "We were a team, but I don't think we made a good team."

She stuck out her lower lip. "Words hurt, pseudo-Dad."

"So do magic energy blasts and explosions produced by conjured soldiers." James yawned. Once he'd unbonded Whispy, a wave of fatigue had crashed over him as if his body needed even more rest after all the adaptations.

"At least it'll be a cool story we both can share. 'Remember that time the Seasons of Rage got dropped in central Texas...'" Harper giggled.

"I meant everything I said earlier," James rumbled. "Don't think you can do whatever you want in the future and run to me for protection. We're not friends. I just didn't think you deserved to die at the hands of the South-guards. I expect people to clean up their own messes, and if you believe any of that shit you were spouting in the core room, it means you need to start taking care of your own problems."

Harper blew out a breath and shrugged, her stubborn smile remaining. "All wise advice. I don't have any reason to complain about how this went down. You could have left me there to die, or you could have killed me yourself at any time. You could have never even come along. For that matter, you could have turned me over to the Southguards. They might not be able to take you in a straight fight, but that doesn't mean they couldn't screw you. There's a reason I'm still going to hide out for a while, even with you giving their lackeys the big 'I'm James Brownstone' speech."

"If they've been around for centuries like you and Shay said, that means they know how to pick their fights so they don't end up getting their asses kicked." James curled a hand into a fist. "And they have to know not to pick a fight with me. My family has a way of ending entire groups who think they can win. I'm not worried about the South-guards. They better hope they never get in my face again, or they can join the list."

Harper rubbed her shoulders. "I almost get chills when you talk like that. What can I say? It's pretty badass. Thanks for everything. When things calm down, maybe we'll see each other again. You're interesting in a weird, judgmental, ass-kicking way."

"I hope not," James replied. "If I never see you again, it'll be too soon."

She let out a merry laugh. "Ouch. You didn't even hesitate when you said that."

"I opened a restaurant and settled down because I wanted a less complicated life," James explained. "You complicate things, and not in a good way. I hope you can clean up your life, but I also hope you do that far away from me. Maybe in a different country."

"Who knows? Maybe I'll open a barbeque restaurant. This courier gig seems a little tired, and I don't think I'll ever be able to take blind jobs again."

"A vegan's gonna open a barbeque restaurant?"

"Sure. Why not? We can have things like barbequed eggplant and tofu."

James grimaced. "That's almost worse than releasing the Seasons of Rage."

Harper offered him a final infectious grin before she

spun on her heel and walked away, waving. "Bye, pseudo-Dad. Congrats—you made me a better person."

James watched her as she walked through the doors to the parking lot. She disappeared into the mass of cars. He was still waiting for his rental truck to be fueled.

Silver party trays covered the table in front of James. Combined, they contained everything a man who had helped saved central Texas needed: ribs, brisket, and pulled pork sandwiches. He'd stopped by Franklin BBQ on his way out of town, and after taking a picture with the owner, had placed his massive order. A good sleep had taken care of his fatigue, but he'd woken up with his stomach growling louder than he did. His only regret was that he didn't have a cooler.

Maybe I should go buy one and come back, so I can bring ribs for my trip back to LA.

James gnawed on a rib as he pondered the possibility. He wasn't sure it was necessary since there were plenty of other barbeque places he planned to hit on his way back, especially now that he'd lost his vegan partner and didn't have to limit his restaurant time to one hour. It might be fun to have ribs in between, though. He tossed a finished rib on his plate, putting aside the cooler idea for the moment.

This is what a road trip is supposed to be, just me hitting the road and enjoying some barbeque. Maybe visiting some friends. I should stop off in Vegas. It's been a while since I talked to Trey face to face. We should arrange some sort of agency-wide mud-

pit battle shit like we did in the old days. It'd be fun. Everything's almost corporate at the agency now.

James grinned, earning a few odd looks from a couple of the other customers but no direct comments. He didn't care. They could just assume he was really into the barbeque. His phone buzzed. He grumbled and pulled it out of his pocket, expecting an unknown number that would turn out to be Harper crying about already being in trouble and needing him to bust into some Nine Systems Alliance cyborg factory.

ALISON BROWNSTONE

James' brow furrowed in confusion as he brought the phone to his ear. "I thought you were getting ready to go on vacation? You shouldn't be wasting time talking to your pse...Dad."

Damn it, Harper.

"Mom's in labor," Alison announced. "She has been for the last twenty-four hours."

James shot out of his seat, the chair falling back and clattering on the floor. A hush fell over the restaurant as the other patrons and waitstaff looked his way, their faces filled with concern.

"It's way early," James shouted. "They didn't say anything about it being this early. Is something wrong with the baby?"

A murmur swept the room at the mention of the baby. Several people clasped their hands and started praying.

"No, not that they've told us," Alison replied. "The doctor says all the vitals are looking good for Mom and the baby." She sighed. "It's just early. We both know there could be a lot of reasons for that, and I don't think freaking out is going to help. The labor may have started early, but it has been progressing slowly. You still can get here if you hurry."

"Great barbeque," James exclaimed to the room. "But I've got an emergency." He reached into his wallet, yanked out a stack of bills, and dropped them on the table to pay for his meal before heading toward the exit, stomping like an angry bull. "Twenty-four hours? Why the fuck am I just hearing about this now? I could have already been back there." He threw open the door, his dark glower parting the crowd in front of him as he headed toward the rental pickup truck.

"Because Mom specifically didn't want you distracted while you were saving Texas from getting overrun by ancient Oriceran invasion artifacts," Alison explained, contrition in her tone. "She specifically said you would come right away, and you would regret it when some town got wiped off the map by the Seasons of Rage."

"That's bullshit," James growled. "My family comes first. *Always*. The entire rest of the world can burn when it comes to my family."

"It was her call, Dad." Alison sighed. "She called me. I happened to be with Rasila. She portaled Mason and me down to LA. I'd have her portal you, but she said she had something to take care of on Oriceran."

"I was done taking care of the artifacts last night," James complained. "You could have told me then."

"Sure, but we didn't know everything was fine until I got your text a few minutes ago."

James gritted his teeth and scrubbed a hand down his face. He reached into his pocket and pressed the open button on the key fob. The door clicked, and he slid into the driver's seat of the red pickup. "Damn it. I was just tired. I figured if anything important happened, Shay would call me, so I didn't bother. It never occurred to me she might go into labor so soon."

I'm gonna miss the birth of my own kid!

"What's your plan?" Alison asked. "You going to use the portal stone Mom gave you? Your best bet is to just portal back to the house, and then you can drive from there. If you were truly magical, we could try to set up some sort of beacon for your portal at the hospital, but I don't think you'll be able to pull it off with that kind of artifact."

"I already used it," he admitted.

"All of this has really impressed on me that I need to improve my technique so I can start portaling."

James grunted. "It's not your fault I'm not there. I'm driving straight to the airport, and I'm going to take the next supersonic flight to L.A." He started the truck. "I can handle a little flying to be there when my kid is born."

CHAPTER TWENTY-ONE

James barreled into the birthing suite, two panicked-looking nurses tugging on his arms. He whipped his head around, seeking his wife, his pulse racing. They'd been so careful, and yet he might have missed the birth of his son.

A pale Shay sat up in the bed, sweat covering her forehead. Alison stood there, holding her hand. A doctor sat on a stool in front of her. They all looked at James in surprise.

"Mr. Brownstone!" one of the nurses exclaimed. "You can't just—"

"I'm not missing the birth of my kid," James bellowed. "I dealt with a lot of shit the last couple of days to help other people out, but now I'm here to see my kid born."

"Shut the fuck up!" Shay screamed. "I'm giving birth here, and the only one who gets to fucking scream is me. Got it?"

The nurses and James winced. Alison snickered and shook her head.

The doctor appeared unfazed. He returned his attention to his patient. "We're almost there. Shay, just keep pushing. Everything's looking great. Both the baby's heart rate and yours are textbook. I know this has been a long, painful process, but we're so close now. Just keep pushing. You can do it."

"Wait." James blinked a few more times and moved opposite Alison to take Shay's other clammy hand. "I didn't miss it?"

"You missed me being in horrible pain for a solid day," Shay muttered. "But you didn't miss the birth. It's like the damned kid was purposely stalling until you got here. 'I want my daddy to see me all slimy when I'm born.'" She related the last sentence in a mocking tone, then grimaced. "I'm really starting to regret deciding on a no-magic, no-drug birth."

They'd had a brief discussion about it. The use of pain suppression magic during birth was becoming more common, even though there hadn't been full studies of the potential side effects on human babies. Their concern stemmed from a different source. Given the unusual parentage of the baby, they couldn't be sure of an unexpected reaction, so they had elected to go all natural.

"I can still do something, Mom." Alison squeezed her hand. "Maybe a spell that just works on your mind."

"I don't know if I'm comfortable with that." The doctor frowned. "Even if you confine it to her mind somehow, there will be downstream biological effects. Neurotransmitter-level changes and that sort of thing."

"I appreciate the offer, Alison, but no." Shay shook her head. "There are too many variables with this kid and he's already coming a month early, so the last thing we need to do is start mucking around with spells."

Alison sighed. "Fine, but the offer's there."

The doctor looked relieved. "I think it's for the best. We're very close now. I know that seems like small comfort given how long this process took, but it'll be over soon, Shay. Just keep pushing and help bring your child into the world."

"How long the process took?" Shay gritted her teeth. "At least when you're shot, it doesn't go on for a day. Why is every Brownstone so stubborn?" She glared at James. "I blame you for this."

Alison laughed. "You've got some stubborn genes yourself."

Shay shot her a dirty look. "Traitor."

James' heart thundered. He barely registered his wife's words. His strength and power might help him annihilate the dangerous magical soldiers of the Seasons of Rage, but they couldn't do anything to help him deliver a baby. All he could do was stand there and comfort Shay. He had to trust his wife, the doctors, and his child.

That's right. Brownstones are *stubborn, and our kid isn't going to let anything happen to him on the day he's born.*

"I'm sorry," he murmured. "I shouldn't have run off on that stupid mission. I should have been here with you from the beginning. We should have just called the PDA."

"If we had done that, the Southguards probably would have gotten their hands on the Seasons of Rage."

The doctor looked at James and Shay, puzzled, but didn't ask for clarification.

Shay snorted before screaming again, then took a few

ragged breaths. "I'm the one who told you to go, and I'm the one who didn't call. I'm also the one who told Alison not to call you. It doesn't matter. You're here now. That's all that matters. And you won't have any regrets about not saving Austin from destruction and shit like that."

"You're crowning," the doctor announced, an excited smile on his face. He cleared his throat. "Though I should warn you, the next stage could take a couple of hours."

"Son of a bitch!" Shay shouted. "That's what you call almost done?"

"I'm sorry, Shay. It might not take that long, but I just wanted to mentally prepare you."

"Stubborn Brownstone here is probably trying to crawl back in." Shay managed a weak laugh. "Whatever. I've been shot, stabbed, fire-balled, death-magicked, and nibbled on by all sorts of weird creatures. A baby's nothing. If I can't handle this, I have no business calling myself a mother. Besides, I get all these great stories in the future when the kid's bad. 'I was in labor for over twenty-four hours, and this is the way you treat me?'"

James and Alison laughed. The doctor let out a quiet chuckle.

Shay tried to manage her breathing. Her face became a rictus of pain as she continued to push.

"I'm here for you, Shay," James murmured.

Hours didn't pass. Stubborn or not, it only took a merciful couple of minutes for the baby to emerge. Nurses and the doctor crowded Shay, blocking James' view.

Damn it. We waited all this time. What is the baby?

A shrill cry cut through the room. A new Brownstone had entered the world. A huge smile took over James' face.

Somewhere, a group of future thugs was shivering in fear, and they didn't even know why.

Tears welled up in Shay's and Alison's eyes. The doctors and nurses wiped the baby down and handed James a pair of surgical scissors. He could barely hear them as they directed him to cut the umbilical cord. They clamped the cord and lifted the baby so Shay could see.

Should I have told her before she saw it?

"It's a boy," she murmured, her cheeks stained with tears. "A beautiful boy."

Alison wiped away some tears. "A little brother, huh? That's perfect."

"A balanced family," James whispered. "A perfect daughter, and now a perfect son."

The tiny pink-cheek boy had a head full of soft black fuzz. He sobbed, squinting and writhing, angry at being born when he was just trying to keep his life simple. Now he'd been thrust into a complicated new world he didn't understand. It was pissing him off.

He was a true Brownstone.

"Welcome to Earth, Thomas James Brownstone," James rumbled. "You're a miracle in more ways than you know, and you have your Brownstone family and all our extended friends and family. We'll be nice and give you a few weeks before we let them all come and pinch your cheeks."

A nurse smiled softly at Shay. "We need to weigh him and take a few other measurements." She gently took the crying baby from Shay and brought him over to the scale after writing a few notes down. "Nine pounds, four ounces."

"Even though he's premature?" Shay asked, her voice quiet.

"It's a healthy weight," the doctor explained. "A bit on the bigger side. He has perfect Apgar scores. We'll need to do a few more tests, but this baby isn't showing any of the symptoms associated with premature birth. If he's this big already, it was a good thing he came out when he did."

Does it mean... It could, but does it?

James took a few deep breaths, trying to control his racing heart. He squeezed Shay's hand. "I need to step out for a second. I need to have a chat with my close friend WD about the baby. Is that okay?"

Shay nodded slowly. "I'm pretty sure we both have the same question.

"I'll stay with her, Dad," Alison offered him a smile. "You do what you need to do. The important part's over."

James stumbled out of the room, only vaguely aware of his surroundings. He had a new child. He had a son, and the boy was completely healthy, despite being born a month early. There was no weird splotches or discolorations. He looked completely human. That wasn't impossible, but it did make him wonder. He found a dark corner in a hallway and reached into his shirt, then yanked the spacer off and grimaced as he bonded with Whispy.

Initiation, the symbiont announced. *What is the nature of the enemy?*

There's no enemy. My kid was just born.

Full reproduction achieved. Any damage to offspring?

The doctor says he's fine, James sent. *Perfect, even.*

That is well inside the expected parameters, Whispy replied.

But they haven't run any genetic tests.

Based on past information, standard human genetic tests will be insufficient to detect the hybrid nature of offspring.

I let it go before, James sent. *But you said something that made me think you'd changed him, maybe modified him. I need to know the truth now. What is he? Is he human? Is he Vax? He looks human. He doesn't have the weirdness like I do on my face, let alone the coloring of a full Vax. I don't care if he's human as long as he'll be healthy.*

Something approaching pride radiated from Whispy.

Because of unfamiliarity with long-term effects of germline modification in hybrid, minimal enhancement was performed, but offspring should have complete compatibility with fundamental symbiont matrix. All existing adaptations will transfer with minimal adjustment required.

James ran his hand over the amulet beneath this shirt. It was a legacy now, something he could pass onto his son. It linked his son to his parents and Father Thomas. He wasn't sure if being compatible with the amulet was a good or bad thing for this boy, but at least, unlike James, his son would understand his true nature and the amulet's nature from the very beginning of his life instead of spending decades stumbling around, hoping for answers.

You're a weapon, but you're also my heritage. Does this mean you'll be serving descendants of mine a thousand years from now?

That probability is currently impossible to calculate, due to insufficient data.

James chuckled. He'd leave the future Brownstones to worry about that kind of thing.

The sound of shattering glass came from farther down the hallway. James narrowed his eyes and walked that way.

A doctor emerged from a side room with a briefcase in hand. A huge fresh yellow stain discolored his white coat. He stared at James for a moment, something odd in his eyes. Fear.

What? Did he just screw something up?

James raised a hand. "Hey, I've got a couple of questions about tests that maybe you could answer. Specifically, genetic tests.

The man's eyes widened, and he sprinted toward a fire door.

"What the fuck?" James muttered.

Engage and kill enemy, Whispy suggested.

First, we have to figure out what's going on. He might just be an incompetent doctor.

James ran after the man. He might be an incompetent doctor, or he might be something far more sinister. No one was going to threaten his newborn son.

CHAPTER TWENTY-TWO

The alarm blared as the doctor rushed out the door, gripping the briefcase tightly. James crashed through the door a moment later, emerging into a side parking lot.

"Hey, Doctor Asshole, stop!" James shouted. "Where are you going? What are you so scared of?"

A security guard holding a stun rod ran around the corner.

Shit. I don't have time for this. I hope he doesn't try to stop me.

"What's going on?" the guard asked.

James pointed to the fleeing doctor. "Do you know that guy?"

"Excuse me, Doctor," the guard called. "I need you to stop for a moment so I can check your..." His eyes narrowed as the man pulled out a pistol. The guard leapt behind the wall as he opened fire. Bullets bounced off the brick wall, sparking.

James slammed his fist into his palm. "Hey, asshole! If you want to shoot someone, try me."

The gunmen turned and bared his teeth. Three quick shots followed. The bullets bounced off James' hardened skin, stinging.

Minor damage sustained to unarmored skin, Whispy reported. *Regeneration in progress.*

"You're gonna stop right now," James shouted, slapping a hand on his chest. "I'm calm despite the situation, but if you end up pissing me off, it's not gonna be a good day for you. You understand?"

The man grunted and emptied his magazine into James. A pile of crumpled bullets soon lay at his feet.

"Don't you get it?" James growled. "That's not gonna work."

The gunman tossed the pistol to the ground and sprinted toward a black sedan across the parking lot.

Panicked idiot. You should have parked your car closer to the emergency door, just in case. It's not like the distance would have mattered if you got out without being noticed.

James pumped his legs, quickly closing on the man, and he tackled the gunman. The other man thudded hard on the ground, his arm smacking the pavement with an audible crack. He screamed in pain and released the briefcase, which skidded a few feet away, the rough surface scratching the leather.

The security guard poked his head around the corner and jogged toward James, his stun rod in hand, a lot more confident now that the other man was unarmed and on the ground with a class-six bounty hunter standing over him.

James reached into the gunman's pockets and yanked out his wallet and phone. He tossed them to the security guard. "You already call the cops?"

"They'll be here soon," the guard replied. He thumbed through the wallet before frowning and shaking his head. "He's got no birthing suite credentials, and I don't recognize him. I've worked here for ten years, and I even recognize a lot of doctors from across town who have visited the birthing center."

James yanked the whimpering gunman to his feet, his eyes blazing. "Do you have any fucking idea who I am? I think you do, but part of me wants to believe you don't. Otherwise, you're a man with a death wish." He shook the man. "Say my fucking name."

"James Brownstone," the man replied. "You broke my arm, Brownstone."

Kill the enemy, Whispy demanded. *Minimize the risk to offspring until tactical self-sufficiency.*

James grabbed the man by the neck and lifted. It'd be easy to crush his throat. "Who the fuck are you, and why are you here? Did you come here to screw with my kid? If you tell me the truth, I won't kill you, but if you lie to me, and I find out you came to hurt my kid, there's no army on Earth or Oriceran that'll be able to protect you."

The gunman's breath caught. His eyes widened. "It's not like that. I'm not here to hurt the kid. I would never hurt your kid, Brownstone. That's suicide. Everyone knows it."

"You have ten seconds to talk about why you're here before I crush your throat," James growled. "My hand's getting mighty twitchy."

Sirens sounded in the distance. The police would be there soon, but James wanted his own information. He would protect his family first and foremost.

"I was paid to get some blood samples," the man cried.

"That's all. They said I didn't even have to be in the same room with the kid. They told me what to look for and got me some codes, and I was just supposed to grab the vials and run. But then I was checking them and I dropped one, and I panicked."

"Blood samples? They haven't even taken that stuff yet."

The gunman nodded, gritting his teeth, his broken arm hanging loosely from his side. His eyes were watering from the pain. "They said to get some blood samples from the Brownstone kid and I'd get paid. I swear no one said anything about hurting the kid. I wouldn't have taken that kind of job, even if they'd paid me a billion dollars."

James tossed the man to the ground and sneered. "I'm only not killing you because it'll make too much paperwork for the police." He nodded to the security guard. The other man nodded back, shaking his stun rod at the gunman.

———

"Mr. Brownstone," the man on the other end answered. "I, as a representative of the Family, am always honored when you call, rare as it is. It also disheartens me that our only lengthy conversation was at your wedding. Word on the street is, your boy was born. Congratulations. A gift will be coming soon."

"You don't need to send me a gift," James rumbled.

"I think I already know, but to what specifically do I owe the pleasure of this call?"

"I've been calling all the local heads because something disturbing happened at the birthing center. Someone was there yesterday, and they were paid to try to steal blood samples from my son. I caught them messing around in a back room, and they shot at a guard and me. They could have killed someone. They could have killed my son."

The mobster hissed. "This is unacceptable disrespect. I take it you killed this piece of shit? I would have."

"Nah. The cops have him and are still interrogating him. He was paid anonymously over the net for the job, but I'm just calling around to make sure you and everyone else can spread the word. Fucking with my son is worse than fucking with me. I'm willing to destroy whole buildings over this kind of thing." James let deep menace seep into his voice. "I trust that everyone understands that?"

"I can't speak for everyone, Mr. Brownstone," the mobster replied. "But *I* understand, which means my people understand by extension. We Family men always understand. I'll spread the word, both to my family and to others outside. I have one question for you, if I may take your time."

"What?" James replied.

"If we happen to find the gentleman who dared disrespect you, can we do what's necessary? Certain things shouldn't be done, and it's important that everyone who swims in our circles understands that."

James took a deep breath. "If you find out who did it, let me know, but I don't care how it's handled. Mostly I just want them to understand they will leave LA, and I want everyone else to understand this is the one and only time I won't kill people over this. Next time, what I'll do will make what I did to the Harriken look nice. This boy is a miracle, and no one will threaten him."

The mobster sighed. "I understand, Mr. Brownstone. We all do what we have to do to protect our families. You have my sympathies for that unpleasantness you encountered on the otherwise joyous day of your son's birth. Have a good day, sir."

James ended the call and grunted. He wasn't worried. He already had a fairly good idea who had done it. According to Tyler's information, a minor Russian mobster had fled his home a couple of hours after the incident at the birthing suite. He was found with his throat slit in an LAX bathroom. His superiors in the organization had noted the man's death in passing when James had called to give the same speech he had just delivered. They explained that some men chose poorly and didn't understand respect, and they too pledged to keep an eye out.

He didn't blame them for not wanting to admit what had happened. Everyone was on edge, and an organization might think James would blame all of them and deliver his unique and explosive brand of justice.

It didn't matter. His son would be coming home that night, where he would be safe with his mother, father, and sister. James just wanted the entire underworld to understand that Thomas James Brownstone was off-limits.

CHAPTER TWENTY-THREE

Baby Thomas lay snuggled on his mother's chest, his eyes closed as he napped. James sat beside them on the couch. He hadn't realized just how much newborn babies slept. Growing up in an orphanage hadn't helped since they'd had few infants at the orphanage over the years. People might be reluctant to adopt older kids, but babies were generally snapped up long before they ended up in an orphanage or foster care.

Shay smiled down at the baby. "I think he looks more like me than you, James. Don't be jealous."

"I'm not jealous. I'm actually happy he looks more like you than me." James ran his hand over his cheek. "I'm an ugly motherfucker."

"I disagree with that, but I'm not going to argue that I'm not hotter than you." Shay grinned.

"At least he doesn't have white hair," Alison joked. "Of course, those would be some interesting genetics, even if I am a magical."

James shrugged. "The way I see it, he'll grow up to be a

handsome ass-kicker, but I don't really give a shit what he looks like as long as he's not a dumbass idiot."

"Isn't that kind of the same thing?" Alison asked.

"Nope. There are subtle differences between being a dumbass and an idiot," James insisted.

"I'll take your word for it, Dad." Alison chuckled.

Shay smiled at Alison. "And I want to apologize to you, Alison. It's been bothering me for a few days, but with everything that's been happening, I didn't get a chance to bring it up."

The young woman's face scrunched in confusion. "For what, Mom? I can't think of anything you have to apologize to me for."

Shay shook her head. "We messed up your vacation. I'm glad Mason's handling it well." She frowned. "Although I wish he'd hurry up and come back from the store with those strawberries. He's a life wizard. He should have just poofed some with a spell."

"Sorry about the strawberries." Alison beamed a smile at her brother. "And the vacation can wait. I have a brother. Sure, he just sleeps, poops, and cries, but at least he's not talking back yet. Thomas is so cute."

Shay stared at Alison. "Getting any ideas?"

James watched her carefully.

"I'm having a lot of trouble figuring out my wedding plans," Alison replied. "I think my kid plans can wait a few more years."

"Just saying. Your life."

"No hurry, Alison," James added. "You can come visit Thomas anytime you want."

Thomas the dog lay at James' feet. He poked his head up and stared at his master.

Alison laughed. "When Baby Thomas gets a little older, he's going to get really confused why he's named after the dog. This might lead to him getting bullied at school."

James snorted. "Anyone who bullies him will quickly learn why you don't fuck with a Brownstone, and he's not named after the dog. You know that. They're both named after Father Thomas. I feel no shame over that. He was a good man, and I'll continue to honor him in every way.

Alison grinned. "Sure, Dad, whatever you say." She turned to the dog. "I know he loves you, boy."

The dog barked and wagged his tail. He'd sniffed the baby a few times but otherwise seemed uninterested. It'd be a long time before Baby Thomas could play with Thomas the dog, so for now, that was enough.

Shay stroked the soft hair of her son, her face utterly content. James had never seen her so completely relaxed and carefree.

"I know you've been keeping it from me, James," she began, "because you didn't want to stress me out, but are we going to have any more trouble with curious fans? I'd rather not burn up my maternity leave killing people, but you know, we do what we have to."

James grunted. He leaned closer to her with a grim look. "The cops, Tyler, and a few others have all told me the same thing. My calls made their point. The entire LA underworld now has an open bounty. They're also apparently doing rotating patrols around our home to watch for anyone suspicious for the next few months."

"That explains all the fancy cars and cops that have

been driving by for the last couple of days." Shay snorted. "I don't know how I feel about gangsters protecting us, but if the gangsters and cops are working together on something, that's probably a good thing."

"Open bounty?" Alison asked. "What's that, exactly?"

James flicked his wrist toward the baby. "Basically, anyone who even talks about harming our son becomes the target of an automatic hit by most of the major underworld groups. They're treating the whole thing as self-preservation since they're afraid we'll destroy them if something happens to the boy."

Shay smiled sweetly. "Well, we would. I will fill the Pacific Ocean with their blood."

James grunted his agreement. Alison offered her own nod.

"Besides, the guy who hired that idiot at the birthing center turned up dead," James continued. "Several other people have already fled town, including a couple of them who were just joking, at least according to Tyler."

"The entire underworld is terrified because of a baby," Shay marveled.

"Good. I like that fear." James leaned back on the couch. "It'll keep everyone from doing anything stupid, but forget about that. It's all been taken care of. Thomas is compatible with Whispy, and that could change things for the future. We need to think about that."

"It changes shit," Shay suggested. "But I don't see how it's important."

"How do you figure? It's damned important. Until a few days ago, I was the only person on this planet who could use Whispy Doom, and now there are two. That also means we have to watch out for the Alliance. I put in a call to Senator Johnston to let him know that if any alien motherfuckers show up, I'll start a War of the Worlds if they so much as sneeze in my son's direction."

"That's fine, but…" Shay tilted her head toward her son. "James, he's a baby. He can't even eat solid foods or sleep through the night. He's not going to work with Whispy for a while, so I think you can pull back on the Tiger Dad super-assault-training parenting worries." She chuckled. "Maybe he doesn't want to kick ass. Maybe he wants to be the world's mightiest gardener."

"He still needs to learn how," James insisted. "He's a Brownstone. He'll always need to defend himself."

"Sure. We'll figure something out." Shay stroked the baby's cheek. "The point is, we have a beautiful, healthy baby boy. We can worry about his tactical training and obstacle courses in a few years, or at least we can wait until he can eat solid foods. For now, the only important thing is for us to be there for him." Tears welled up in her eyes. "We're a family, all four of us. Three of us didn't get to have the kind of family experience we might have wanted, but we found each other. Now we can work together to give Thomas a perfect life." She kissed the sleeping baby's forehead.

Alison walked over to hug her mother and the baby. James pulled them all into a hug.

"We're Brownstones," he declared. "We'll always be there for one another."

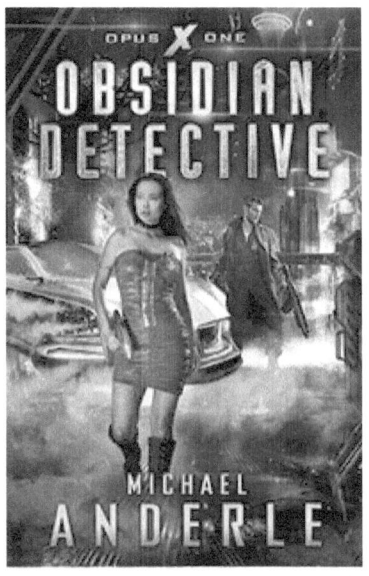

Pre-order now to have the book arrive on your Kindle November 1st.

Two Rebels whose Worlds Collide on a Planetary Level.
On the fringes of human space, a murder will light a fuse and send two different people colliding together.

She lives on Earth, where peace among the population is a given. He is on the fringe of society where authority is how much firepower you wield.

She is from the powerful, the elite. He is with the military.

Both want the truth – but is revealing the truth good for society?

Two years ago, a small moon in a far off system was set to be the location of the first intergalactic war between humans and an alien race.

It never happened. However, something was found many are willing to kill to keep a secret.

Now, they have killed the wrong people.

How many will need to die to keep the truth hidden?

As many as is needed.

He will have vengeance no matter the cost. *She will dig for the truth. No matter how risky the truth is to reveal.*

Coming November 1st from Amazon and other Digital Book Stores

Thank you for reading all the way back here! (*AND* the book, let's not forget about the book.)

So, I've recently been back to Jessie Rae's for some BBQ (awesome stuff, just saying) and had a chance to remember when I first sat down at the red and white checkered round table in their little second dining room. That fateful day when I penned the information that would become, in time, *The Unbelievable Mr. Brownstone*.

And his love of barbeque.

I've read many of the reviews, and I appreciate all of them. However, I get a (tiny) sort of sadistic glee when you relate how while reading these Brownstone stories, you find yourself NEEDING to either smoke some meat or go find an open restaurant to pick some up.

Bringing joy, sadness, laughter, hunger—pretty much any emotion really—to a reader is a way for us to know that we authors are doing our jobs.

Plus, my "evil" plan to encourage more BBQ-eating around the world has come to fruition. Perhaps it is a tiny amount (more like a square-foot garden vs. a few acres) but still, I was able to encourage others to partake in the joy that is smoked or grilled meat.

(*Editor's Note: On September 6, I was being driven to our hotel in Budapest, Hungary, and we passed Bubba's BBQ. It's all over!!*)

Mmmmmm.

On another note, when I was at Jessie Rae's, Mike's mom, who occasionally runs the register, was there and mentioned an event that happened last July, so about two months ago.

One of you awesome readers had come by and enjoyed the BBQ and asked Mike Ross (Mr. BBQ himself of Jessie Rae's) to sign a book. Mike was a little surprised, but he did sign it, and promptly apologized for getting BBQ sauce on the book.

His mom said he was honored, and this is a call out that if you go by, feel free to ask him to sign your book if you want. I appreciate Mike for giving us a shot when using his establishment in *Brownstone*.

It's fun to see his mom's eyes light up. She never thought a bunch of readers would come to Las Vegas and go visit a BBQ place.

I'm really happy to say that YOU have made a difference, and Mike says that *Brownstone* is hands down the best marketing his BBQ place has...

GO US!

I placed this in the back of Animus Book 9 and I think you might enjoy it.

"The Author would say thank you for reading this book...if the author was around." John turned around. He was standing on the sidewalk, the trees shading both sides of the street as he tried to find the voice among the shrubs in old Ms. Benjamin's yard.

He spoke aloud. "Come again?"

"I said..." the voice replied. John looked down. At his feet, about as high as his Converse high tops, was a small...

Fairy? *A lawn fairy?* He got closer and knelt. He then noticed the razor-sharp teeth. The fairy continued speaking. "...that the author would have said *thank you* for reading the book."

"What book?"

"Unbelievable Mr. Brownstone."

John thought about it. "I haven't read a Brownstone since... Uh... He got married to Shay. Last I read was the latest *Animus*." John didn't like the look on the little guy's face. "Did I miss one?"

"You missed *two*, actually." He put his hands on his hips and glared up. "You call yourself a reader?"

"I've been busy. You know," John jerked a thumb at his blue Nike backpack, "college."

"Not an acceptable excuse," the small fairy answered. "In fact, there *is* no excuse. It is what we told the Author before we had our final negotiation. He promises he won't be tardy again."

"Whatevs," John stood up. "I've got to go, I'll get to it when I get to...OUCH!" John's hand swept down, meeting the foot he was lifting as he slapped the little guy off of his ankle, rocketing him into the grass.

There was blood running down, soaking his sock. "Dude, why the hell did you bite me?" he asked. John noticed the little guy's maniacal grin as he wiped a bit of skin and meat off his lips. The fairy climbed out of the grass to get to the sidewalk.

"How the hell did you get such a big chunk out of my foot, ya ass?" John knelt again, moving his sock to catch more of the blood.

"Dinner shouldn't call me names!" the lawn fairy hissed, his voice going up an octave.

"Dinner?" John stared at him, "I'm not your dinner, you masochistic mosquito. I'm a hundred times your size, and..." John noticed the tall grass starting to move in Ms. Benjamin's lawn. Like something—or several somethings—was coming through it. "I'm, uh..."

"You...are...*dinner.*" The fairy smiled once more, showing the red on his teeth. John's blood. "At least the Author was smart enough to negotiate. You just called me names..."

John jumped up, turned, and sprinted away.

Forty-five minutes later, a dog started sniffing a blue backpack five houses down, which was lying on the sidewalk.

John was nowhere to be seen.

WE HAVE TWO MORE ANIMUS *BOOKS COMING...*
Don't let the Lawn Fairies catch you missing one.
Once they finish with John, you might be next...

If you haven't read
The Unbelievable Mr. Brownstone,
we suggest you try it.

If you have read all of
The Unbelievable Mr. Brownstone,
and all of Animus...
You are safe.

For now.

OTHER SERIES IN THE ORICERAN
UNIVERSE:

THE DANIEL CODEX SERIES
I FEAR NO EVIL
THE UNBELIEVABLE MR. BROWNSTONE
ALISON BROWNSTONE
SCHOOL OF NECESSARY MAGIC
SCHOOL OF NECESSARY MAGIC: RAINE CAMPBELL
FEDERAL AGENTS OF MAGIC
THE LEIRA CHRONICLES
REWRITING JUSTICE
THE KACY CHRONICLES
MIDWEST MAGIC CHRONICLES
SOUL STONE MAGE
THE FAIRHAVEN CHRONICLES

OTHER BOOKS BY JUDITH BERENS

BOOKS BY MICHAEL ANDERLE

For a complete list of books by Michael Anderle, please visit

www.lmbpn.com/ma-books/

All LMBPN Audiobooks are Available at Audible.com and
iTunes. For a complete list of audiobooks visit:

www.lmbpn.com/audible

CONNECT WITH MICHAEL ANDERLE

Michael Anderle Social
   Website:
   http://www.lmbpn.com

Email List:
   http://lmbpn.com/email/

Facebook Here:
   https://www.facebook.com/OriceranUniverse/
   https://www.
   facebook.com/TheKurtherianGambitBooks/